The Bishop Riders

The Bishop Riders had terrorized the valley nearly fifty years earlier and in a shoot-out and fire the gang had been killed – except for the Bishop himself. Now rustlers and killers were threatening the range again, so the word went round that Bishop was back. It was into this land of fear and suspicion that Nevada Jenkins and Tim Greer rode.

They would soon become deeply involved in all the killings until, finally, it was down to them to put an end to the strife and solve the mystery. But they had a long struggle before them, and bullet and knife would take their toll.

The Bishop Riders

Graham Hawk

A Black Horse Western

ROBERT HALE · LONDON

© 1952, 2003 Vic J. Hanson
First hardcover edition 2003
Originally published in paperback as
The Bishop Riders by V. Joseph Hanson

ISBN 0 7090 7276 7

Robert Hale Limited
Clerkenwell House
Clerkenwell Green
London EC1R 0HT

The right of Vic J. Hanson to be identified as
author of this work has been asserted by him
in accordance with the Copyright, Design and
Patents Act 1988.

All characters and events in this book are
fictitious and any resemblance to any real
person or circumstance is unintentional

Typeset by
Derek Doyle & Associates, Liverpool.
Printed and bound in Great Britain by
Antony Rowe Limited, Wiltshire

CHAPTER ONE

The hoofbeats of racing horses were muffled by the base symphony of the storm, and the riders were almost upon the cowhands and the herd before they were spotted. As if to herald their dramatic entrance, the thunder crashed once more and the clouds were torn wide open by a jagged gash of lightning, spotlighting fitfully the dark riders and the huge, hooded figure of their leader.

'*The Bishop's!*'

The night-rider's voice rose to a scream which ended in a bubbling gasp as a slug caught him in the throat. The oncoming riders were shooting with deadly precision as they encircled the herd and its luckless attendants.

The leader drew back his steed a little and watched.

Horse and rider looked like a carven statue, huge, terrible; a hooded spirit watching his masked minions at their devilish work.

A madly-galloping horse went past him, its rider screaming as, one foot in the stirrup, he was dragged along, twisting and turning in a feeble effort to get free. The hooded man drew a gun from beneath his cloak, levelled it and fired twice.

The dangling figure bounced as the frenzied horse went faster. But there was something different about the figure now; it was devoid of life as a badly-stuffed doll.

Another rider broke through the encircling ring and rode straight for the hooded man, then swerved, lifting a gun. The leader bent in the saddle a little and the black horse bounded forward. The cowhand fired, then fired again frenziedly. The horse squealed with pain as the heavier beast hit it broadside.

The cowhand reeled in the saddle. He saw eyes blazing at him from the shapeless black mass which was the other man's head. Righting himself, he fought a superstitious dread that threatened to paralyse his gun-hand. As he raised his gun he saw the muzzle of the other one looming into his face and he felt the last pangs of a terrible frustration before the slug obliterated everything for him. The hooded man shot the horse, too, so that it fell atop the body of its master.

The night-riders were outnumbered by three to one. Also, sodden and wretched after an hour or more of driving rain, and hampered by dripping slickers, they had been taken pretty much by surprise. The raiders moved with the ruthless precision of a bunch of shock-troopers. They fired at the bigger targets, the horses, then finished off the unseated men in an almost leisurely fashion, in most cases with a single bullet in the side of the head.

Maddened by the shooting and the smell of death – on top of the rain and thunder and lightning – the old leader-bulls began to move. The rest of the herd streamed after them, beginning to bunch as they gathered speed.

A night-rider, trying to make a getaway on foot, screamed once before he disappeared beneath the flying hoofs. One man made a flying leap and landed astride a racing steer. From there he began shooting and yelling defiance at the raiders. He brought one of them down. Then his cries changed to screams. Lightning illuminated his contorted face, the eyes staring, the mouth yammering as incoherent words bubbled from it. His body was stretched upwards, as if he was trying to stand up on the steer's back. But he could not do so because his legs were being slowly crushed by the solid mass of bovine flesh which milled all around him. His body jerked as bullets thudded into it, then it flopped forward as if it were hinged at the waist. A few moments later it disappeared altogether.

All resistance was at an end; the raiders raced alongside the maddened cattle, their leader keeping pace with them now, shouting orders, drawing steadily ahead. As he reached the head of the herd he began to shoot, bringing the leaders crashing forward so that those behind piled against them. The steers began to swerve, began to slow down. The men turned them in the required direction.

The storm eased a little. The cool breeze took the rain away with it and the dark, scudding clouds dissolved before the brilliance of the skies. The range became bathed with starlight. It had the appearance of a small battlefield, tragic and pitiful. The remnants of the little war lay scattered, marking the trail of the victorious army. Men and horses lay in grotesque positions. Three dead steers were in a line, an almost identical space between each of them. Then there was a pile of the beasts, four in all, tumbled together as if awaiting the butcher's knife.

The breeze soughed through the tall wet grass, which glistened in the starlight or lay flatly like a stagnant river where the herd had passed.

'I guess we're on *Snake W* land now, Tim,' said the older of the two horsemen.

He was lean and rather ancient looking. Long, grey hair straggled from beneath his battered sombrero. His face was mahogany-coloured with little wrinkles of humour around his bright, grey eyes. His clothes were plain and well-worn, the ingrained dust of many trails in every crease. His companion was a young man of about twenty, fit-looking, lean-faced. Like his pard, he wore a Colt revolver in the holster slung from his leather cartridge belt.

The old man went on: 'It's good to be back in the of place. I warn't no older'n you, Tim, when I left it.'

Tim grinned. 'I bet you were a salty little skunk.'

'Such lip!' snorted the old-timer in mock rage. Then his face became serious. 'Though I guess I was kind of salty at that. You had to be in this territory.'

The other sat erect in the saddle and looked mighty interested. 'Why – was there plenty of action?'

'I'll tell a horse!' said the old man. 'Range warrustlin' – the Bishop's riders—!'

'The Bishop's Riders?' echoed Tim. 'I've heard you speak of them before. What were they?'

'I'll tell you all about it later. Right now it looks like we're gonna have company.'

The young man followed his companion's gaze. The approaching bunch of riders came on fast. They were almost upon the wanderers when the old-timer yelled:

'Brad Turner!'

The big, elderly man who led the bunch reined his horse in front of the pair.

'Nevada Jenkins!' he exclaimed. There was surprise in his voice. But it was harsh and his face did not exactly light up in welcome.

He held out a huge hand, however, and, with a dour look on his face, the old timer shook it. The two elderly men seemed to be weighing each other up a little quizzically. Brad Turner had a broad, lined face and grey eyes, which were as cold as Nevada's were warm and humorous. Brad's iron-grey hair was very long and thick, so that his battered Stetson looked a little small for his head, yet made him seem even taller so that he towered over the rest of his men. They, seven in all, bunched themselves a little behind him. They were all young and hard-featured, and they watched the newcomers with a studiously-veiled interest which seemed to have a hint of menace.

Nevada exchanged glances with his young pard and then made rather belated introductions. 'Tim, I want you to meet a very old friend o'mine, Brad Turner. Brad, this is my side-kick, Tim Greer.'

Brad nodded to Tim and grunted a howdy. Tim made as if to offer his hand, then, seeing that the big man's attention was turned from him again, let it fall with a tiny slap. He could almost feel the veiled eyes of the other man boring into him.

'What brings you back in this part of the country, Nevada?' asked Brad.

'Figured I'd like to see the old place again. It's been a long time – a long time. Figured I'd like to show it to Tim, too. We've punched steers all over, but he ain't seen this part o' the country before.'

Brad sat erect in the saddle. His men were like sentinels around him. The big man seemed to be making up his mind about something. His head was bent and his eyes were shadowed a little. It was as if there was a film over them. They looked at Nevada and Tim, but they looked past them, too, at something the others could not see – at something, maybe, that only Nevada could share with him.

Finally he raised his head and looked at the old man, and his eyes seemed to have softened a little. 'You're welcome,' he drawled. He half-turned in the saddle then and introduced his men one by one, and they, too, seemed to relax a little, to look more like ordinary hard-working cowpokes again, as they made their howdies.

Brad said: 'You boys see any more men as you rode this way?'

'No,' replied Nevada. 'We didn't see a soul – except a few cows.'

'You didn't see or hear a moving herd this morning or maybe last night?'

'We haven't seen anything half like a moving herd since we left Kansas City three days ago, and the only folks we've seen were the old Mex and his wife at Pedro's Casino and a couple of drunken wranglers.

'Which way were the wranglers heading?'

'This way, they said, but they were mighty slow and their main cargo was half a barrel of red-eye, so we left 'em behind. What's the—?'

Unconsciously it seemed, Brad cut Nevada's sentence short, saying, 'We were just looking for another bunch of my boys who are out here some place. I thought you might've seen 'em.'

'Nope. Not a sign of 'em.'

Brad seemed to be thinking again, his leonine head slightly bent. He said, 'Well, look, Nevada, if you an' your pard would like to ride aways with us we shall probably meet the boys, and we can all ride back to the ranch together.'

'A little more ridin' won't hurt us none,' said Nevada.

But, that riding they did not have to do, for at this juncture one of the men who had gone forward suddenly called, 'Here come the boys now!'

The newcomers, five in all, came on fast. They were led by a lean, dark man, who reigned in a few yards away from Brad Turner and the two strangers. His eyes watched the latter, and Tim Greer thought they were like the eyes of a mountain puma. The other four men grouped themselves behind him, hard-faced cowhands all of them, watchful, too.

'Well, Matt?' said Brad Turner, harshly.

By contrast the lean dark man's voice was almost silky.

'We've been right into the hills. The ground's hammered. We thought we'd picked up the proper trail once. Then, whether it was the right one or not, we lost it on the hard rock.'

The man called Matt stopped talking, and again he looked at Nevada and Tim. So Brad introduced them, and introduced him as Matt Jarando, his foreman.

Jarando said howdy and his men said howdy, but nobody shook hands.

'Did you two gentlemen come through the hills?' queried the foreman.

It was Tim Greer who answered the question this time and there was an edge on his voice.

'We did, *friend*. Why?'

The word 'friend' was like the tiny flick of a whip and Jarando's face darkened a little at the sound of it. The blood pulsed beneath the dark skin, but the face did not change expression and the voice was as silky as ever as he said:

'Did you see any men or any cattle, any marks of camp fires?'

Tim Greer said, 'We didn't see a thing, friend. We've already told your boss that—'

'You came through the pass?'

'Yeh.'

'Which pass?'

Nevada interposed hastily, 'My pardner doesn't know this territory. It was the Widow Pass.'

'You *do* know this territory, hey, old timer?'

'I was born a few miles from here,' said the old man softly.

'That's quite a coincidence, ain't it?' said Jarando. 'Where've you been all these years?'

He was taut in the saddle as if awaiting the old man's angry retort. Old Nevada was a man of peace, but whatever he meant to say was left unspoken, as Tim Greer kneed his horse gently forward until he was directly facing the foreman.

Jarando had to look at him instead of the old man.

'Is somep'n bothering you, friend?' Tim Greer said softly.

Jarando's yellow-flecked puma's eyes flickered, then became still. His left hand held the reins, his right rested on his saddle. His lean body seemed to slump a little, to relax, but his eyes did not blink. Eyes could give so much away to an opponent, a gunfighter; eyes could telegraph a movement even before it was made; eyes could make the difference between victory and annihilation, between life and death. The two men measured each other and their eyes told each other nothing. It was another movement which brought them out of their half-trance. Brad Turner rode forward a little and the tension was eased as he said:

'Nevada Jenkins is a very old friend of mine.'

'Is he, boss?' said Matt Jarando.

His voice was no longer silky. It was a little husky. And although he was not looking at Tim Greer any more – was not looking at anything in particular, except maybe inwards so that the eyes were a little smoky, there was something in them which was not very pleasant.

CHAPTER TWO

'Let's get back to the ranch,' said Brad Turner and he turned his horse about.

They rode and the men began to talk loudly and rather self-consciously like men going into battle. The tension seemed to hang over them like a cloud all the time and the two newcomers were acutely aware of it.

Tim Greer particularly could feel it and could not help being antagonized by it. The men talked to him but they said banal things which he hardly heard. Matt Jarando was riding behind him now but Tim could almost feel those queer eyes boring into him. Presently the foreman rode past without looking at him and joined Brad and Nevada up ahead. He did not stay long there however but wheeled away and began to circle the bunch. He was as restless and dangerous as a mountain-cat.

Tim Greer loved fighting. Even the companionship of the peace-loving Nevada could not kill that urge. He did not like this tension, this mystery, it piqued and antagonised him and in some way, perhaps inevitably, that antagonism had become centred on the foreman. Although Tim Greer would have been the last to admit it there was something very much alike in the two of them.

Out of earshot of the rest Nevada was talking gently to his old friend. 'I thought Trinity Valley would be peaceful and restful now. Maybe that's why I came here. I'm getting old, Brad: I'm all through raising hell. I guess I want to spend my last days where I spent my first, and in peace.' His voice had a questioning tone.

'Well,' said Brad slowly. 'If it's peace you want, Nevada, you'd better leave this range.'

'I figured there was trouble. Maybe big trouble, huh?'

'Yes, big trouble. The Bishop's Riders have come back.'

'Bishop's Riders come back!' echoed Nevada incredulously. 'Why – they couldn't! The Bishop's bin dead years.'

'Maybe it's his ghost then like some o' the punchers say. Some of 'em are lighting out like scared rabbits. But ghosts don't lead bands of rustlers who kill men, and stampede cattle. The Riders ran off my prize herd last night an' killed nine men; leaving no more trace than a sidewinder.'

'Coming back here reminded me of the old Riders and the hell they used to raise,' said Nevada half to himself. 'I was mentioning them to my pard just as you came along. Now it seemed almost like yesterday. But them days are over and done with—'

'They've come back, Nevada.'

'But they can't – are you sure—?' The old man was almost incoherent; his voice faded.

Brad let him be until he spoke again and his voice was normal though still thoughtful. 'So that was why everybody acted so strange – no wonder – and that foreman o' yours carries that man-sized chip on his shoulder.'

'Matt's a kind of a queer cuss – but he's the best ramrod in the territory. I should warn you pard not to needle him too much.'

'Tim only retaliates in kind,' said Nevada almost primly. 'Anyway, though he's only a younker he can take care of himself, believe me.'

'He seems a decent young cuss at that,' said Brad in a conciliatory tone. 'How did you come to meet him, Nevada?'

'Well, if you're interested—'

'I am.'

So once more the old man delved into his warbag of memories; and came up with one of his prize ones for the benefit of his old friend. He told of a night in Abilene in the heyday of that blustering hub of the cattle-kingdom when the rain poured and Texas Street was a river of mud and the saloons and honky-tonks and casinos were packed to suffocation. Abilene now was a wan copy of its old self; long-eared burroes drooped before sagging false fronts and flies buzzed over the shredding bones of the dead horse on Texas Street – but that night there was no hint of such a seedy fate, there was only riches and life and death and glory. Nevada was getting on and he had seen it all: it had made him a little cynical. He carried his roll in his body-belt weighted beneath a Colt forty-four.

He wanted everything that Abilene could give him and if that included gunplay, well, he'd take that, too, and his chances with it.

He did not fight unless he was provoked, his cynicism forbade even that. But he was provoked when he saw a drunken brute thrashing a boy with an iron-weighted trace. He knocked the man down. But the brute did not choose to stay down and the lead began to fly. Before Nevada knew what had happened he had killed the man and a scared kid was clinging to his pants' legs.

'That's how I met Tim,' he said. 'The dead man had kept a sporting-house. He had been the protector of Tim's mother – what a grand old Southern term that word 'protector' is – he protected her so well that she died young. Tim could only just remember her dying. All he knew about his real father was that he had been a gambler. He had gotten himself killed – probably across the tables – and left his wife penniless. After his mother died the boy was dog-of-all work around there – until I came along. He stuck to me like a clam. I didn't want him at first but, by Jimmy, I've been glad of him since. He saved my life a couple of times. That kid was tempered in the fire an' it's made his nerves like steel!'

Nevada's voice tailed away. Brad said: 'Here we are – home.' Nevada came to himself and looked at his old friend. He had heard the sadness in his voice, and now he could see it heavy for the moment in the unguarded face before it became set and expressionless once more.

They reined in at the corral and a couple of youths came forward to take their horses. They too had the same hard, wary, half-fearful look. The rest of the riders streamed in and began to dismount, milling, a little uncertainly it seemed. They gathered against the corral fence and more than one of them made hasty movements as two other men suddenly rode fast around the corner of the ranchhouse.

As they reined in Brad Turner went forward to meet them, making a sign for Nevada to follow him. He introduced the old man to burly blonde-haired Nolly Travers of the neighbouring *Big Bend Ranch* and his little foreman, Pete Parsons.

Nevada said: 'You'll be ol' Gimpy Travers's boy, I guess. I was mighty sorry to hear about your dad's death.'

'I was his adopted son,' said Nolly. 'He often talked about you, Nevada.'

'Bad news, Nolly?' said Brad.

'Well, after hearing what happened on your range I've got to admit it could be worse. They ran off fifty-odd head o' my stock but I only lost one man: "Peso" Maroni. We buried him this morning.'

The *Snake W* men had gathered near. A half-breed, Pedro, sighed loudly.

'*Madre de Dios*! Poor Peso! Like me he knows it is useless to fight the Bishop. He was planning to leave today.'

Nolly Travers said suddenly, 'I can't stand this any longer, Brad. I guess I'll sell to those Ace people.'

'I wonder if they're still keen on buying,' said Brad Turner softly.

That day in the bunkhouse Tim Greer heard the legend of the Bishop's Riders who had terrorized this valley half a century ago. They attacked silently, killed, burned, and robbed, then vanished as mysteriously as they came. Terrified settlers began to say that the Riders were not human. The Bishop, as they called the hooded leader, was an arch-fiend leading his minions in wholesale slaughter which would mean eventually the extermination of every living soul in Trinity Valley. Many of the settlers left – Indians they could understand and fight but spirits were a different matter altogether.

The remaining homesteaders decided on one last desperate stand. The Riders, growing careless, attacked the ranch buildings of the biggest spread in the territory. The alarm was given, armed men rode from every corner of the valley, and the Bishop's Riders were trapped in the very ranch-house they had taken. After a pitched gun-battle the enraged homesteaders set the place on fire and, proven human after all, the Bishop's Riders either ran out and gave themselves up or perished in the blazing inferno. The giant leader was not captured so it was naturally assumed that his charred bones were among the other remains.

Pedro spoke up. 'I still say that even if his Riders were human the Bishop was not. Now he has returned to repay the valley for the scorn it heaped upon him.'

'Don't talk so hydroprodious, Pedro,' said another man scornfully. 'Ef'n the Bishop's still alive, he must be a mighty ol' man now.'

'You do not understand,' said Pedro, his dark Indian eyes glowing strangely. 'Many strange things happen in these lands before you white people came!'

Meanwhile, in the ranchhouse Nevada began to learn a few more things too. They all stemmed from the question he asked Brad: who were these Ace people Nolly Travers planned to sell out to?

Brad Turner said, 'Some months ago I had a visit from a man named Gowans, a representative of a big Chicago syndicate who call themselves the Ace Development Company. Seems like they're taking over territory right an' left all over the West an' they want Trinity Valley an' the spreads in it. I don't know what he told the smaller homesteaders, but some of 'em sold out mighty quick. Three calls this Gowans *hombre* made on me. Each time I gave him a flat 'NO!' The last time he turned quite nasty. He said his employers were used to getting what they wanted and were very annoyed when they didn't – but that in the finish they always did. I told him to keep off my place, or next time I'd fill his hide full o' buckshot.

'All the smaller spreads have sold out. All who're left now are myself, Nolly Travers of the *Big Bend*, an' Bill Lakeman of the *Circle U*. A month ago the Bishop's Riders started their games – small games – until this last terrible night!'

'Yuh think the Bishop's Riders have sump'n to do with the Syndicate?' said Nevada.

'It's possible ain't it? I don't believe in ghosts anyway.'

'Neither do I,' said Nevada. 'Some o' these Eastern syndicates are trying to grab the 'ull damn West.'

'But do you think they'd go to those lengths to get what they wanted?'

'I dunno.' Nevada shook his head. 'I just don't know! I guess I'm getting old. I guess things just ain't what they used to be. The old codes don't hold good anymore – men are slaughtered without having a chance to defend themselves. Shooting a man in the back ain't the crime it used to be. The world's full of horse-thieves and quacks who call themselves businessmen. And it seems to me that some of them will stoop to anything.'

'But this! – it seems fantastic.'

'It ain't any more fantastic than the thought of the Bishop's ghost rampaging around.'

Nevada was sitting near the window. He leaned forward as he heard the sound of rumbling wheels and clattering hoofs from outside. Brad rose and came slowly across to the window.

The cart went slowly by, a single man erect and still on the box up front. A large tarpaulin sheet had been thrown over the back completely covering it but bulging strangely here and there. The cart passed away from the two men at the window and they saw the thing dangling past the tailboard. It was a man's arm, a white hand hanging at the end, fingers half-clawed swaying gently with the movement of the cart.

Brad Turner turned away violently, almost knocking over a chair.

'Nine men – Nine good men!' There was a break in his voice.

'Shot down, trampled. It's fantastic – but Nevada, it's true!' The last words were like a cry of anguish as Brad slumped back into his chair. He rose again almost immediately as there was the clattering of hoofs outside. Once more half-fearfully he crossed to the window and looked out.

'It's the sheriff and his deputies,' he said.

Sheriff Francis Lord was a well-preserved man of middle-age. His well-built figure was tightly encased in black broadcloth. He had a shoe-string bow, a pearly-grey ten-gallon hat, chased riding-boots of the finest leather, and a black moustache with beautifully-waxed points. He could have been a river dandy, a big shot gambler, even some kind of flashly businessman – But he wore his star right and prominent on his fancy vest and a pair of Colts with walnut handles chased in silver, slung low in tooled leather holsters tied to his thighs by whang-strings.

'Nothing, Brad,' said the Sheriff. 'No clues. No nothing. It's like chasing gophers. We've been way out – for just nothing.'

He could maybe have been a salesman too. He talked real pretty and had a deep resonant voice. Nevada Jenkins found him a little hard to figure. He could be just a fashion plate. But did dummies wear guns that way? He could be a real salty *hombre*.

'What we want is a necktie party,' said Brad. 'A necktie party to keep riding – till we catch up. Till we—'

'Riding?' interrupted the sheriff softly – 'Where to?'

Brad expelled a gust of breath which was like a huge sigh of agony. He was back to earth, corralled. 'Have a drink, Sheriff,' he said.

'I guess we'd better be riding, Brad. Thanks all the same.' The sheriff turned his horse and led his men away.

Brad watched them in silence until they were a mere puff of dust on the shimmering range. Then he turned to Nevada and said, 'Guess I was kinda peevish but that panty-waist gets in my craw. Though he was right, I guess. There's nothing—' he spread his hands in a pitifully eloquent gesture, 'just nothing.'

'Kind of a queer sheriff,' probed Nevada.

'Yeh, he's kinda new too. Only been here six months. Brought in by the State Marshal. We'd got nobody to nominate after old Al Brodie retired. So—' Brad spread his hands again. 'Not that I've got anything against the gent. He seems zealous enough. He's had next to nothing to handle till just now. Trinity Valley was a mighty peaceable place till the Bishop's Riders started on the rampage again. Though it ain't so, it can't be—' Brad broke off again: he was just a simple cattleman, he knew there were many things he could not understand.

CHAPTER THREE

The range had been newly washed by the storm of the previous night and on the following one the darkness fell gently. There was a moon as well as the stars and even the breeze was gentle. It was not a night for thieves and murderers. It seemed that nothing could happen on a night like this; but the ranchmen of Trinity Valley were taking no chances.

Patrols were as thick as burrs in a buffalo's hide. The only fear was that, if anything happened, would they be in the right place at the right time. The range was big beneath the moon, so very big.

A man lay in a hollow at the edge of a clump of cottonwoods with his hands behind his head and thought how big the range was and the sky.

He had a blanket across his legs and, a few yards behind him beneath the trees was the smouldering remains of a fire. His horse, ground-hitched there, was champing contentedly.

The man felt rather than heard the faint vibration of the ground beneath him. He rolled onto his side and pressed his ear to the coarse grass. The feeling became a sound, spasmodic drumbeats, and he knew there were cattle nearby, and maybe horses, too. He sat up and tested the direction of the wind. It was travelling past him and out that way.

A faint sense of unease held him now. The wind seemed to be playing tricks. He threw back the blanket and, sitting up, raised his knees. He reached for his boots and began to put them on. One went on easily but the other gave him trouble. He rose to his feet, cursing the boot as he tried to cram his foot into it. A sound from his horse made him turn quickly, almost falling.

A voice said, 'You won't need no boots, pardner.'

The lopsided figure blurred into action and a gun boomed from among the trees, a tongue of flame spitting viciously. The man with one boot staggered and cursed again. Something fell to the ground with a soft thud and he grabbed his right arm with his left hand. He stared into the darkness and cursed softly, precisely and with feeling.

'Stay right where you are, pardner,' said the voice again. It had gone nasty now.

'Hold it,' admonished another voice sharply and the man with one boot had a crawly feeling in his belly. Had that second voice prevented him from stopping a couple of slugs right where that feeling was?

He pushed his luck, for that was the way he was made. 'Dirty belly-crawling skunks,' he said.

The men began to move out of the trees and gather in a half-circle around he with one boot. He counted them one by one. He counted seven. He tried to weigh them up in the darkness. He got the feel of them and the feel was not good. He said, 'Well, what do you want. All I've got is my horse, my gun, my pants—'

Nobody answered him. A high voice sniggered and another one, the second one maybe, said 'Shut up!' It seemed to come from the lean man who stood next to the stocky one with the gun.

'Maybe we'd better have a necktie party right now,' said the high voice again and a man danced forward dangling a coiled riata in his hand.

The lean man swept a long arm outwards. There was a dull smack and the man with the riata fell on his back. He sat up and looked around owlishly. The man with one boot began to chuckle.

The lean man started forward, his hand dipping. The stranger made a similar movement: it was useless and he remained poised. Then as the lean man came nearer he side-stepped and made a little skipping movement and swung a fist. But the lean man was fast too. He jerked his head back and the blow missed him. He lunged forward with his own fist and it was loaded. The long barrel of the gun caught the stranger in the stomach and he gulped. He weaved a little, tried to cover up.

He felt the steel bite into his shoulder; the men were all around him now and the blows came from all sides. The voice said 'Hold it!' again and those were the last words he heard.

There were no words when he came to, just dull sick pain, a smell; and a movement which was not made by him yet seemed a part of him. The smell gave him his first clue, it was pungent and unmistakable. After that it was easy for him to deduce that he was slung across the back of a horse and his arms were tied in front of him around the beast's neck so that his face was almost buried in its mane. His feet were lashed under its belly. There was a rope around his neck too but he could not figure where the other end of that might be. It wasn't too tight – he could still breathe – but it was tight enough. He knew what could be done with the other end of that halter: it was not a pleasant thought.

He raised his head a little but he could not see much. It was still dark and men were riding all around him. The creak of saddle leather and the jingling of harness were familiar and beautiful sounds but they did little to soothe him now.

He tried to reckon up the damage. The shot which had been fired had only stung his arm. It was probably only a crease and was not bleeding now though the flesh was stuck uncomfortably to the sleeve. His lips felt puffy where somebody had smacked him; he had been hit in a few places in his face. He had a bruise on his shoulder where the lean fellow had pistol-whipped him, but he figured he could still move his arms. And his legs, too, if he ever had the chance.

'The North line-hut's the nearest,' said a voice which he figured to be the lean fellow's.

That was what he had to look forward to: the North line-hut. Until then – what could he do? The answer was: just nothing. He let his head rest on the horse's neck. He had had harder pillows, it gentled the throbbing of his head. He let himself go, let himself be rocked by the motion of riding and he realized he was astride his own beast. This fact unaccountably heartened him. At least he had one friend left, if only a four-footed one. He tried not to be cynical about this. He let himself doze.

He was alert when the horses stopped. Things happened quickly. The rope on his hands and feet were cut viciously but the one at his throat was tightened so that he almost choked. He tumbled from the horse. He staggered to his feet. The pressure was slackened a little, but he found he could not speak. He gulped air. He was half-carried, half-shoved into darkness and knocked down onto a hard wooden floor.

'Where's Pete?' said a voice. 'Doggone it, where's Pete?'

A lucifer was scratched and light blossomed to become fully-fledged as somebody lit the hurricane lantern in the low roof. At that moment the stranger was lifted and slammed back against the wall. He still had only one boot. He blinked in the light and began to curse again. He had a sweet and versatile vocabulary.

He had a little leisure now to look around him: as everybody else was doing, presumably looking for Pete. The place was like any of hundreds of Western line-huts. A table, two chairs, a pot-bellied stove, a dresser with utensils, a couple of bales of wire in a corner, a bursted horse-hair sofa.

Pete, it seemed, wasn't around any more so the men turned their attention to the prisoner. Other men filed in and said there was not any sign of Pete outside either. They filled the little cabin and they began to advance on the stranger, the lean dark man leading them. The stranger looked into the latter's eyes and knew that here was a man without mercy. He had met such men before, had seen the same light in their eyes. They had something inside of them which drove them to do things at which lesser mortals would blanch.

The lean fellow had his gun in his hand again; and his weapon was not the only one in evidence. Whatever was eating these people they certainly looked like they meant business.

'What's your name, stranger?' said the lean man softly.

'You can call me Pete.'

Another man sniggered and the stranger watched the lean man's eyes. He saw that certain light in them and he braced himself. Why did he always have to be so funny? But the lean man seemed to hold himself in and nothing happened.

The man just went on talking.

'The name isn't important I guess. Where do you hail from?'

'The Pecos.'

'Just the Pecos, huh?'

'Just the Pecos. I've been around.'

'What are you doing in this neck o' the woods.'

'Just riding. I get around.'

This seemed to amuse the lean fellow. He smiled a thin-lipped smile which did not show his teeth. He said: 'You were scouting maybe.'

'Maybe. Scouting for a job.'

'Cowhand?'

'Yeh.'

The last reply had another effect on the lean man. He lashed out with the gun. If the stranger had not jerked his head back the gleaming barrel would have taken the tip of his nose off.

'Matt!' said somebody.

'Matt is it,' said the stranger. 'By Gad! I'll—'

'Tie him up!' said the lean man. He stood away from the stranger who called himself Pete, who was not trying to be funny any more, who was suddenly transformed.

He was lean, too, but very broad of shoulder. His shoulders sloped and his arms were so long that they gave him a slightly ape-like appearance. Beneath the recent scare his face was smooth and immobile, an aquiline face with a deeply-cleft chin and thin quirking lips which were both humorous and bitter at the same time.

It was his eyes that gave him away now. They did not blaze with fury as any other man's might have done. They were like thin chips of ice and a light smouldered deep in them. Oldtimers used to say that that half-hidden glow was the light of the soul: this man had the killer urge in his soul and now it smouldered there for those who understood it to see.

Matt Jarando understood it and it enraged him. He waited till the man was trussed up, upright against the wall, then he hit him twice in the face.

The man's head jerked. Blood trickled down his chin. He called Jarando a name.

The *Snake W* foreman had worked off his spleen. He was silky again. He said:

'Where's the rest of the your bunch? And maybe you know where Pete is too.'

'I don't know what you're after. I know nothing—'

'Light the fire. I'll make him talk.'

'Look, Matt—' The man who spoke was the stocky one who had fired the first shot that night. The lean man silenced him a gesture.

'Do as you're told,' he snarled.

A man bent over the stove. 'The wood an' paper is already laid. I wonder why Pete—' He left his sentence unfinished. He scratched a match and lit the paper at the bottom vent. In a few seconds the stove was roaring.

'Look, Matt,' said one man plaintively. 'Why'n't we quit playing around. Why'n't we just string him up.'

Jarando turned on him with such violence that he recoiled.

'Hanging one man won't bring nine men back to life. Nine we want – more than nine. He's got to be made to talk—'

'Sure, Matt – sure.'

But the foreman had forgotten him already. Head bent, he was communing with himself. He cast sly glances at the prisoner as if they two were all alone. Finally he seemed to come to a decision. 'There should be a branding iron in that dresser,' he said. 'Hand it to me.'

Nobody said anything. A man opened the dresser cupboard and brought out the iron and handed it to Jarando. He crossed to the stove and lifted off the top plate quickly, wincing at the heat. He let the plate fall to the hearth. Its clatter was startling in the stillness.

With a slowly deliberate movement he thrust the iron into the flames.

'Put some coal in,' he said, and one of the men picked up the bucket and set to doing the job. The handle of the branding-iron stuck up like some kind of symbol. Jarando turned away from it and went back to the prisoner. He stood looking at him for a moment. Then he reached out, grabbed a handful of shirt and pulled.

The cloth tore with a noise which seemed unutterably loud. The man's bronzed chest was revealed, a powerful chest sprinkled with brown hairs which glistened here and there a little in the light. Jarando went on tearing until the man's stomach was bare too and his shirt was hanging around him in tatters. Jarando poked a finger in just above the navel.

'That'll be the first place,' he said. 'Then I'll work my way upwards.' '

He looked around at his men, impersonally, as if they were an audience. And that was the way they looked. Nobody spoke. They had no individual thoughts any more or, if they had, were scared to voice them. They were an audience waiting with bated breath for the performance to begin – knowing that they had never seen a performance before quite like the one they were going to see now. Unless—

Jarando turnd his head again. 'Are you going to talk – Pete?' he said.

'You're crazy.'

The stranger's voice had a little tremor. The high-voiced guy sniggered again with such suddenness that the sound had the effect of a gunshot. Men started. Jarando whirled with murder in his face. The offender faded to the back of the cabin.

Jarando strode across to the stove and, with a gloved hand plucked the branding-iron free. The end, bearing the rather intricate *Snake W* mark, glowed red.

'Ain't that pretty!' said Jarando.

He turned about and advanced on the trussed man, holding the iron in front of him like a lance pointing straight at the naked belly. The stranger shrank back against the wall, his head bent as if he could not bear to look at the glowing brand. No sound came from him. There was no sound except that of Jarando's measured footsteps.

CHAPTER FOUR

The hot iron was almost touching the naked flesh when everybody became suddenly aware that the stranger had been foxing. He took even Jarando by surprise.

He lurched forward, twisting his body at the same time with an almost superhuman effort. There was a sudden sizzling noise and a smell of burning cloth, then the iron was knocked flying from the ramrod's hand.

Another man squealed, as much with shock as with pain, as the hot iron struck his arm. Then it fell to the floor to sizzle the boards. So violent and sudden had been the trussed man's manoeuvre that Matt Jarando was sent sprawling by the lurching body.

'Are you all crazy?' yelled the man who called himself Pete. 'Don't a man get a chance around here?'

The sick tension had been broken; he was playing a long shot. Cursing, Matt Jarando rolled on the floor among the feet of his men. Pete crashed there too, trussed like a turkey but still lashing them all with his tongue.

It was at this juncture that the door flew open and Nevada Jenkins and Tim Greer came in. They both had their guns out. 'Jumping Jiminy!' said the old man. 'What's going on?'

Everybody began to talk at once. Matt Jarando climbed to his feet. After this anti-climax he seemed temporarily deflated. But when the prisoner said plaintively 'Why don't somebody pick me up?' the foreman turned and kicked him in the ribs.

'That wasn't nice,' chided Nevada. His gun winked in the light as he jerked it.

Tim Greer moved forward a little. He did not jerk his gun but it was pointed straight at the foreman's chest. Jarando glowered hate at him but had an uncomfortable feeling that the younker would be glad to begin shooting if anybody started anything. Tim Greer was lined up with the desperate men in this room; Jarando had a funny feeling about it. It was the stocky man who helped the prisoner to his feet and even brushed him down absently.

'This *hombre* was scouting for the rustlers,' blurted out Jarando.

'Can you prove that?' asked Tim Greer.

'He said he was scouting.'

'I said I was scouting for work,' said the prisoner. 'As a matter of fact I was scouting for a ranch called the *Big Bend* owned by a Mr Nolly Travers. A man told me there'd be a job waiting for me there.'

'What man?' It was Greer who spoke again.

'A man I met in a saloon at Solomon Creek. I guess he was some kind of agent for Mr Travers.'

'A likely story,' sneered Matt Jarando. 'Anyway, why didn't you try us with that one in the first place?'

'I don't like being pushed.'

The stocky man came forward with an open claspknife and, rather sheepishly, cut the stranger's bonds.

The man flexed his hands and stamped his feet. 'Mr Pete Garner of Texas thanks you, gentlemen,' he said. 'Many lands has he visited in his role of wandering minstrel but never before has he experienced a welcome such as this.' He bowed a little awkwardly. 'The initiation is now, I presume, concluded.'

'I guess the best thing we can do is take him to Nolly Travers and see what he says about it,' said Nevada Jenkins. The cavalcade mounted and rode away from the hut. Pete Garner, unarmed, but sent in front. He was silent now and very good. He knew that if he made a false move a dozen bullets would thud into his back.

When he did make a move it was not exactly a false one, but still it might have been his last.

He reined in his horse and pointed at something in front of him. 'Would that be the missing Pete?' he said.

He sat his horse then, immobile and erect and it was Tim Greer who dismounted first and ran to the figure huddled in the grass.

He rolled the body over, 'It's Pete all right,' he said. 'His throat's been cut from ear to ear.'

Everybody was stunned for a moment and, strangely enough, nobody attempted to attack the man who called himself Pete Garner. Even Matt Jarando was strangely subdued. The middle-aged Pete who lay there in the grass has been his friend, perhaps his only real friend on the *Snake W* spread. He dismounted and Tim Greer helped him place the body across his saddle. Then the foreman said harshly, 'Bud, Lanny – you come with me. We'll take Pete home.'

The stocky man and the weedy one with the high-pitched voice detached themselves from the bunch. The two parties separated, Nevada and Tim going with the larger one.

On the edge of Big Bend land they were held up by a heavily-armed bunch of night-riders. They had to do quite a bit of explaining before they were allowed to pass. As they approached the ranch buildings four more armed guards stopped them. These were a mite more friendly, except to the stranger. They said things had been pretty quiet up till now. The news of Peter Sanderson's death, which might have been accomplished by a ghost, sent one of them galloping back to warn the boss. The *Snake W* party followed at a slower pace.

Nolly Travers was a bachelor and for a man of his lusty age seemed to live pretty quietly. He had been on the point of retiring. Clad in a dressing-gown he came out onto the verandah of the ranchhouse to greet his visitors. He looked very big and menacing there in the darkness. His men, many of them hastening from the bunkhouse, formed a half-circle behind the *Snake W* boys and their prisoner.

'What's the trouble now?' said Travers. He sounded a little peevish, even a little scared.

'Pete Sanderson's been kilt,' said one of the men, a high note to his voice.

'The Riders—?'

'We don't know yet,' said Nevada Jenkins. 'Could we have a little light, Mr Travers?'

Travers turned his head, looked back into the darkness and bawled, 'Yate.'

A figure materialized from the gloom then faded again as Travers said, 'A lantern.'

The men waited. Nobody said anything. Light blossomed back there in the house. It grew. An old Indian shuffled out like a scared ghost. He held a hurricane-lamp aloft.

Both Nevada and Tim dismounted and, at a sign from the latter the man who called himself Pete Garner got down too. Nevada had his gun out. He jerked it. 'Get on up there, stranger,' he said.

Garner approached the steps with Nevada and Tim behind him. None of the other *Snake W* men spoke or moved. Now that Jarando was not with them they did not seem to mind the oldtimer taking the initiative.

The three men moved into the aura of the lantern-light. 'Stay right there, Mr Garner,' said Nevada.

Garner stopped walking. He was face to face with Travers. Nevada and Tim took their stand at the top of the steps, one against each post. 'What's this?' said Travers.

The lantern wavered in the old Indian's hand. The rays illuminated for a moment the still silent men grouped out there then moved away. Grotesque shadows danced on the log walls. 'Bring that light nearer,' said Nevada.

The Indian started. Then he shuffled nearer. Travers and Garner faced each other, their faces garishly illumined now. Travers opened his mouth to speak but again Nevada beat him to it.

'Do you know this man, Nolly?'

'Can't say that I do.'

'No, maybe not. But he says your agent sent him here to work for you.'

'My agent—'

Nevada interrupted Travers, saying quickly, 'What did you say that agent's name was, stranger?'

'I didn't. He didn't tell me his name.'

'What did he look like?'

'Dark stocky fellow. Fortyish. Wearing sideburns and a bushy black moustache. Dressed in store-clothes. Carried a fancy derringer in his belt.'

'That's a good description of Mike Emms,' said

Nolly. 'I haven't seen him for a couple of days. Where did you meet him?'

'Solomon Creek.'

'Could be.' Travers sounded a little stupefied.

There was silence for a moment. Then Nevada said, 'Well, Nolly, will you vouch for this gink? Will we leave him here?'

'I don't want any man,' said Travers. 'Emms had no business sending a man here without letting me know.'

'That's the way it is, is it?' said Pete Garner softly.

'That's the way it is,' said Nolly flinging his arms out suddenly. 'Why should I vouch for you. I don't know you. For all I know you are working for the Riders – even though you did meet Emms in Solomon Creek: that ain't so far away. For all I know you did kill Pete Sanderson. If you didn't who did? My men haven't seen anybody—'

Nevada broke in on the tirade saying gently, 'What will we do with him, Nolly?'

'You can do what you damwell please with him. But take him away from here. I've got enough trouble.'

'Looks like you're a reg'lar little orphan of the storm, pardner,' said Nevada.

It was an unfortunate remark: one of the men seized upon it. 'Yeh, of last night's storm no doubt, only that time he wore a mask. I vote we string him up.'

An altercation broke out. Things did not look so good for Mr Pete Garner. Then another bunch of

Big Bend men rode into the yard: an escort for Brad Turner.

'What's going on?' boomed the *Snake W* boss. 'Where's this man you picked up?'

Everybody started to talk at once but finally when he could make himself heard above the din Brad said, 'All right bring him back to the ranch.'

Then with a curt 'good-night', to Nolly Travers he led his men away.

One of the *Big Bend* men remarked, 'Well, if the sonofabitch did kill Pete Sanderson it's fitting the *Snake W* folks should handle him, I guess.'

'He'll get no mercy from Brad Turner,' said another. 'That man's all rock.'

'What you all standing about for?' Nolly Travers suddenly bawled. 'Get on about your business.'

The men faded away. Nolly went back into the house, grumbling under his breath, 'Worry, worry – all the time, worry!'

CHAPTER FIVE

The sun-motes danced through the open bunkhouse window. They were gentle on the face of Tim Greer as he slowly opened his eyes. He was alert in an instant, looking about him. He let out a little sigh when he realized where he was. Just another bunkhouse. He was on yet another payroll.

He lay for a while and let the things come back to him. Yeh, the things were a little different here. Idly he watched other men wake and begin to rise. His pard, Nevada, grinned at him. But nobody else was grinning and there was none of the early morning chaff which is the usual custom in bunkhouses from the Rockies to the Rio. A heaviness lay over the place and even the sunshine could not dispell it.

Tim knew hard glances were thrown at him as he swaggered to the door. He went through, and closed it behind him. A man, stripped to the waist, was bending beneath the first pump. A wedge-shaped body as brown as the soil of the Dakota hills – except in one place. Tim felt his flesh crawl a little; he could only remember having that feeling once before. From the man's right shoulder, running diagonally across his body to a point above his left hip was a wide white scar. As he splashed his face with water, and the lean muscles rippled the white scar rippled too, like a living snake.

The mutilated back glistened with water as the man straightened up and reached for his towel. He turned and Tim saw the deep chest sprinkled with fine brown hairs. 'Good morning, Mr Garner,' he said.

One of the man's bare feet went slap on the ground as he straddled his legs. One hand balled into a fist, the other drew the towel away from the lean brown face and those cold, blue eyes looked into Tim's. Then just as quickly the tension had gone, and the man who called himself Pete Garner was smiling that crooked smile which held much yet held nothing.

Tim Greer's smooth features were immobile. If he felt any surprise he concealed it admirably. He went to the next pump and took off his shirt.

Garner said, 'I'll be seeing you,' and moved off around the corner of the bunkhouse.

Tim pondered if any of the other men knew about him and what they would say when they did. He was about to shove his head under the pump when a voice spoke behind him. He whirled, adopted a defensive attitude.

Brad Turner stood there, his feet encased in carpet slippers. 'Have you seen Pete Garner?' he asked.

'Yeh, boss, he just went round the corner.'

'The damn fool,' said Turner and he, too, disappeared.

Greer made a gesture which might have meant anything. Then he proceeded with his ablutions.

Other men began to trickle around back to wash. Nobody seemed to be saying much, and Greer did not bother to eavesdrop. He dried himself and went around the front of the bunkhouse once more. There was no sign of Pete Garner or Brad Turner. He saw a couple of horsemen approaching across the range and he stood and watched them.

They came nearer. Almost unconsciously Tim shaded his eyes with his hand. He held his hand there, he craned his neck, he seemed mighty interested in what he saw. The two riders veered towards the ranchhouse. One was slight and wore a hat that seemed a little too big. The other was huge and hunch-shouldered. It was the former, however, who interested Tim most. Finally he reached his conclusion; yeh, it was a woman all right. A young one too and from where he was, a mighty pretty one. With a trim figure in blouse and riding-pants and high-heeled boots. A beautiful seat on the silver-grey pony. With brown windblown hair cascading from beneath the huge brim of the hat. Because of the hat he could not see the face – but it just had to be pretty. He saw Brad Turner come out on to the verandah to meet them. Again he wondered what had happened to Pete Garner.

He started as he heard a sound behind him. He turned to face Nevada: what was the matter with him, was he getting jittery, or had the sight of a woman gotten him into a moondaze? The two visitors had left their horses and gone into the house. But Brad Turner came out onto the verandah again. 'Nevada,' he called. 'Tim – come on over here.'

Tim obeyed with alacrity. Nevada bumbling along behind him said, 'What's the rush, young 'un?' They stamped onto the verandah and Brad led them through the screen door and into the big living-room.

The Venetian blinds were still drawn and the shady centre of the room was barred with sunshine while the deeper shadows clustered in the corners. The two visitors were sitting still and silent by the window. Tim had a fleeting glimpse of the craggy shadowed features of the man then he was looking into the face of the girl, which seemed almost ethereally pale in the half-light.

Their looks met for only a fleeting instant for Nevada suddenly bounded past Tim and obscured his view. At the same instant the craggy-featured man rose to his feet. The two oldtimers clasped hands and shook each other by the shoulders. They did not say anything for a bit. Then it was

Nevada who spoke first saying, 'And so this is Julia?'

The girl had risen, too. She took the old man's hand and smiled. She was bareheaded now and Tim, who had manoeuvred himself into a favourable position once more decided that she was indeed pretty. Hell, no, she was beautiful!

Nevada said: 'The last time I saw you, young lady, you were no bigger'n handful o' dimes.'

'That was in Kansas City, Julia,' said the other oldtimer. 'You were only three. I took you there to see the fair.'

'I can almost remember it,' said the girl. 'Yes, I'm sure I remember it.' She gave a little ripple of laughter.

'Of course you remember it,' said Nevada. 'That was when you met me. You couldn't forget that,'

The two old men chuckled softly and the girl threw back her head. She laughed richly. Then the laugh died to a gurgle and she was looking at Tim and he found himself feeling acutely uncomfortable as if in laughing she had been in some way mocking him. She was about his own age, maybe a little younger.

Nevada said jovially, 'Tim, I want you to meet another very old friend o' mine: Bill Lakeman. And this is, as you'll have gathered, his daughter Julia – Folks, I want you to meet my side-kick Tim Greer.'

Tim remembered hearing Bill Lakeman mentioned before. He was the owner of the *Circle U* spread. His hand was very big and he had a grip like a vice. By contrast his daughter's grip was soft but firm. It was velvety and very fleeting.

Silence fell on the room and a sudden gravity too. Abruptly Brad Turner crossed to the window and raised the blind. The sunshine came in with almost savage force.

'Sit down Nevada, – Tim,' said Brad.

The partners took chairs side by side and Tim found himself facing the girl. Her hair had copper glints in the sunlight and, as far as he could make out, her eyes were green.

The talk became grave and Tim realized the girl was like her father's right-hand man. She was no longer smiling and there was the same resonance in her voice as in the old man's, though hers was softer and wholly feminine. They were shocked at the tragedy which had overtaken the *Snake W* and would be at the funeral that afternoon along with everybody else. In the meantime some plan had to be made to take care of the living.

The Bishop's Riders had paid the *Circle U* a visit, too, on that tragic night. They had run off about fifty head of cattle but there had been no killing.

'I'm afraid my men, being only a few, didn't stop to argue,' said Bill Lakeman drily. 'I guess it's lucky for them they didn't.'

'The skunks certainly made a clean sweep,' said Brad Turner. 'How do they do it?'

The girl, Julia, said: 'They must have a huge force if they split up into sections to take care of each ranch!'

'But the Bishop himself was seen with them at each place,' said her father.

'Any man could wear a hood.'

'That's so. But judging by the times, approximate anyway, I think they do the jobs one by one.'

'They always hit me the hardest,' said Brad Turner.

'Probably because you're nearest the hills,' said Bill Lakeman.

'All this surmising won't get us anywhere,' said Brad Turner. 'We've got to be ready for them next time. The question is: what to do?'

'I vote we bring gunmen in from outside.'

'That's a big thing, Bill. You'd never know who you can trust.'

'I think Nolly Travers is already doing it.'

'No? – He told me he intended to sell out!'

'Maybe he's changed his mind. Anyway, it might be only a rumour I heard,' Bill Lakeman shut up, clamped his lips tight as if he figured he had already said too much.

'Strange,' murmured Brad. 'Strange.' Then he livened up. 'We'll pool our men and we'll ask for more help from the law.'

'That dressed-up galoot—'

'Oh, father, I'm sure the sheriff is doing his best,' interjected the girl.

Tim Greer felt a pang inside of him. Did she go for that panty-waist?

Things were left kind of hanging. They promised to see each other again that afternoon.

Then Bill Lakeman and Julia took their leave. Nevada and Tim went to the chuckhouse to get some chow. Nobody said anything when they entered. Maybe that was because everybody was busy eating. But there was an atmosphere too, the partners sensed it, and it was not exactly friendly.

After chow everybody made for the bunkhouse, there to await Matt Jarando with the orders for the day. The foreman had a little cabin on the edge of the ranch buildings. Sometimes he had his breakfast in the mess-hut with the rest, sometimes he had it right at home. Nobody had seen him around yet this morning.

He was not there awaiting them in the bunkhouse. But somebody else was. The man called Pete Garner sat in the corner bunk, the one which had belonged to Pete Sanderson. Maybe it was only a coincidence that he was cleaning his rifle, and that his Colt, obviously newly-polished, lay on the blankets beside him.

Everybody glanced at him as if they could hardy believe their eyes. But nobody went too near to him. Even those who had bunks nearby, skirted him widely though a little clumsily. The only people who spoke to him were Tim and Nevada and their greetings were curt. Everybody stared at him like he had two heads when he spoke up in a drawling voice. 'I hope you gentlemen don't mind, but I'm liable to be around for awhile. Mr Turner has put me on the payroll.'

Nobody had anything to say to that. The tension

was almost unbearable. It was broken, or maybe heightened, by the sudden appearance of Matt Jarando.

He flung the door open and stood in the aperture. He seemed to be tensed and, with his leanness, for a moment to tower over everybody else. His eyes ranged the room and finally came to rest on Pete Garner.

He spoke then, addressing the whole room loudly, but with his eyes still fixed on the new man. 'Heard the latest, boys? This sidewinder's one of us now. He's the boss's white-haired boy. He even had his breakfast in the boss's kitchen—'

'It was the boss's wish,' drawled Garner. 'I wanted to come to the chuckhouse—'

'Yeh, an' I suppose it was the boss's wish you have Pete's bunk too?'

'It was. It was the only empty bunk. He had fresh blankets put on for me.'

'Good,' said Jarando. 'Fine.' He wagged his head. His voice rose still higher, as if he was haranguing a huge crowd. 'Folks, all you've got to do to get a job on the *Snake W* is kill one of their men – shoot him, tramp all over him, cut his throat, do it any way you like. But just so long as you do it good Mr Turner will give you a job – and the dead man's bunk to boot.'

Pete Garner rose slowly. 'You've no call to talk like that, friend,' he drawled.

Matt Jarando started forward. His men made way for him.

'Get away from that bunk,' he said. 'Get away from Pete's bunk.'

'Watch him, Matt,' said somebody. 'He's got a gun.'

Jarando was beside himself with rage, but he had guts. He went on and, as he did so, Pete Garner laid down his rifle and left his Colt behind and came forward to meet him.

'You don't know what you're talking about, friend,' he said mildly.

They both moved fast then. Doubtless, Garner had been just foxing again. And Jarando, who probably hadn't even noticed that the man was unarmed now, was reaching for his gun even as Garner moved in.

Jarando's gun went off, but prematurely, the slug burying itself in the boards as Garner's fist exploded on the foreman's jaw.

Even as he was falling Jarando, his eyes blazing insanely, was trying to bring the gun level. Garner hit him again, in the middle, then again, a chopping blow on the right bicep. The gun clattered to the floor. Jarando, twisting, fell almost on top of it. Garner's next move was to kick the gun out of reach.

The rest of the men moved back with an inherent sense of fair play which they themselves would probably not have been able to explain. They formed a rough circle.

Garner's face was a little paler now and his eyes were almost hidden. He stepped back and waited for Jarando to rise. The foreman got up slowly, warily, watching his man from under lowered brows. The insane look had gone from him, leaving his eyes dull and smouldering. He made a lunge, then stopped dead, feinting. Garner shot out a feeler, missing. Jarando leapt, his arms opening wide. When they closed he had Garner in their grip. Garner went slack but the manoeuvre did not work. Jarando almost threw him off his feet. Garner tried to drive in body-blows but they were fluffed: he was too close. He began to play Jarando at his own game. They wrestled like a couple of grizzlies. They were pretty evenly matched. They swayed then crashed to the floor together: men stepped back hastily as the two rolled.

Jarando was on top. He was feeling for Garner's throat. The latter had hold of his wrists and was trying to force those clawing hands away. But Jarando had all the weight behind him, and plenty of leverage. Garner's eyes began to start a little with the effort; sweat beaded his forehead; he knew what would happen once those fingers got a good grip. Jarando wouldn't let up until there was no life left beneath them. Garner groaned, dropped his hands, went suddenly slack. Jarando, who had been using all his weight, was thrown violently forward on top of his man. Garner's viciously upthrust knees completed the manoeuvre. Jarando was catapulted away. But even as he hit the floor he was twisting and, though he followed up his advantage quickly, Garner missed him.

For a moment the two grown men kicked around on the floor like a couple of babes. Then they reached for each other again. Garner got a hold first. He got hold of the front of Jarando's shirt with both hands and began to lift him. He rose himself at the same time. Jarando tried to grab him but was off-balance and could only make ineffectual scrabbling movements. Garner hauled him all the way then let go with one hand, balled it into a fist and hit Jarando three rapid blows in the face. The sounds were very nasty in the stillness.

Jarando, spitting blood, began to fight back, driving in low blows. Garner gulped and let him go, lashing out again with both fists. Jarando went down. For a moment he lay spread-eagled, his face staring upwards. But Jarando was not as bad as he looked. He sat up. Then he uncoiled the whole of his length like some kind of spring, stretching full length, flinging himself at his opponent. They stood toe-to-toe in the centre of the floor and swapped blows until a voice bawled, 'Stop it! Doggone you, stop it!'

Nobody had heard the door open. The boss stood there. He had a gun in his hand and he looked very ready to use it. Jarando flung a last swinging blow at Garner, which missed. Then he drew back, even a little sheepishly. The two men stood panting, their arms dangling, ape-like, and looked at Brad Turner. Everybody looked at Brad Turner.

He said: 'I'll shoot the next man who starts anything. I mean that. I guess maybe there'll be plenty of fighting for you sooner or later without you fighting among yourselves. Those of you who were out with the herds yesterday I want out there again. The rest of you clean yourselves up. Have you forgotten what you have to do this afternoon?'

This was merely a gentle reprimand. But it affected the men more than curses would have done. They remembered what they had to do that afternoon. They had to pay a last homage to nine of their comrades.

'We'll finish this business at some other time,' drawled Pete Garner.

'We'll finish it all right,' said Matt Jarando cryptically. It was as if the two men had been nursing their hate for years before this climax.

CHAPTER SIX

The funeral was held in the neighbouring small town of Bancoville, so-called because it had grown from a stores, honkytonk and sporting house kept by a gent known as 'Banco' Charlie. The old dice cheating game, Banco, was Charlie's favourite lay. He was playing it at the very hour, nay the very minute of his death – when an enraged 'sucker' plugged him plumb through the heart.

During the ensuing melee the 'establishment' was set on fire and burnt to the ground. From its ashes rose a small settlement of clapboard, tin and dobe huts. Charlie was immortalised by a wag who christened the place after the luckless gambler's favourite pastime. The name stuck.

Now Bancoville had a couple of saloons, a Wells Fargo branch, a smithy, an all-purpose stores, a chapel and all the rest of the paraphernalia of a mushroom township – plus a population, static and floating, which made its living in various ways in and around the place.

This day the town had a floating population

much larger than usual: sightseers for the most part, some of them from as far afield as Kansas City. The newspapers had blazed the story of the fabulous and awe-inspiring Bishop's Riders and their nine – ten, counting a greaser – victims. To some minds this shindig in once-peaceful Trinity Valley, was the beginning of the greatest things since the Lincoln County range-wars. This applied in particular for the journalists who were as thick as buzzards around carrion. They had gobbled up all they could find, fact or fable, about the Bishop's Riders, and they wanted more.

They accosted cowhands, they tried to get at their bosses. Cowboys are gregarious creatures but they have a few codes that might seem a little queer to city people. They live hard and many die hard, too, but they believe in the mystery and dignity of death. A reporter was quietly manhandled by a bunch of them, which served as a lesson to the rest to sing small while the funeral was under way.

As was the custom nobody rode. The men walked up the dusty street in their newest high-heeled riding boots. The dead, except for three of them who had families, were buried in a communal grave. The officiating clergyman was Ep Cornwall, known locally as 'the Professor'. For once he was cold sober, and his concluding eloquence when he called down 'the wrath of the Lord on the fiendish murderers' had never been bettered even by his bell-like tongue. There were many wet eyes among the menfolk and stifled sobs from the women.

Standing beside the grave as the earth fell into it Tim Greer raised his head and looked across to meet the eyes of Julia Lakeman. They were dry and wide and brilliant. They looked at Tim yet did not seem to see him. Her face was pale and set. Tim felt a strange catch in his throat, taking his breath for a moment as he looked at the cameo-like beauty of that face. Then she was turning, taking her father's arm, and moving away.

At a touch on his shoulder Tim came out of his half-trance and joined Nevada and Brad Turner. He saw Pete Garner standing nearby, a strange set look on his face which, because of the ironical curve of his lips, had in it a suggestion of mockery. Matt Jarando was nowhere to be seen.

A man suddenly accosted Brad Turner. A little man in store-clothes and a very Eastern-looking slouch hat, a red face like a bloated turkey-cock and a quiff of black oiled hair which came low over his forehead. He was perspiring freely and his jowls trembled a little as he spoke.

'I'd like to convey my deep sympathy, Mr Turner,' he gabbled. 'Truly. Sincerely. It's terrible, terrible. I'm going to ask my firm to take me away from this place. Whatever may have gone before between us I feel for you – I feel for all of you, deeply: in case I don't see you again I want you to know that.'

'Thank you, Mr Gowans,' said Brad Turner softly.

The man bobbed his head, turned and vanished in the crowd.

'Gowans?' echoed Nevada.

'Yeh. Mr Gowans of Chicago – and the Ace Development Company.'

'And he didn't make you an offer,' said Nevada slyly.

The three men went on down the street. A little way in front of them were Julia and Bill Lakeman. Beside the old man's lumbering walk the girl's carriage was graceful and as light as thistledown. Yet Tim Greer, watching, saw something faintly voluptuous in it too. Julia was no milk-and-white prissy miss, but a lusty frontierswoman.

The girl and the old man got into their rig which stood outside the stables. Their heads turned simultaneously as they looked towards the saloon on the opposite side of the street. Then old Bill made an abrupt gesture and the girl whipped up the horses. The rig clattered away down the street in a cloud of dust.

The three *Snake W* men heard the sound of the altercation as they approached the saloon. 'If that isn't Matt Jarando I'll eat my sombero,' said Brad Turner without humour. He pushed open the batwings. The other two followed him in. They were just in time to see the *Snake W* ramrod struggling in the grip of four men while Nolly Travers sagged against the bar with his hands to his throat. The *Big Bend* boss straightened up and staggered across the room. He went past the three men without seeing them and disappeared in the street.

'Matt tried to strangle him,' volunteered somebody. 'They're both drunk.'

The two men who had been holding Jarando let him go. He staggered across to the bar. 'Give me a drink,' he said thickly, 'before I shoot the place up.'

'Don't give him any more,' rapped Brad Turner and strode forward. The barman hesitated. Jarando grabbed for him and missed. Then he turned.

'Hulloa, boss,' he said.

'What's the matter with you: are you completely crazy?'

'Can't a man have a little drink if he wants to?'

'A little drink! Do you call this a *little* drink? At a time like this, too. What were you and Nolly fighting about?'

'He said somep'n I didn't like.'

'Is that all?'

'They seemed quite friendly at first,' said a man behind. 'Then Nolly started loud-talking like he usually does when he's had too much. Talking about all kinds of people.'

'Matt – you know Nolly is a blabber-mouth: he never means any harm.'

'I heard him say something about Pete Sanderson,' said the informant behind.

'Dead men can't defend themselves,' said Jarando owlishly.

Then he glared at the man behind Turner and

snarled. 'You mind your own damn business or I'll take care o' you, too.'

'You will huh?' The man started forward and another brawl was only averted by Tim and Nevada getting in the *hombre's* way. He bobbed around, trying to dodge them, shouting insults all the while at Jarando as Brad Turner led the teetering foreman away. This was the nonsensical climax to the tragic day.

Jarando, quite docile now, was taken home and put in his bunk. He even managed to mumble an apology for his actions at such a time. Then he fell into a deep sleep. Nevada Jenkins looked down at his form, powerful and catlike even in slumber. 'He must have thought a heap of that Pete Sanderson,' he said softly.

The man tossed and moaned in a tortured sleep and silently they left him. As they turned away from the cabin door Brad Turner was riding across the yard. He had been to see Nolly Travers. He dismounted and Nevada told him that the ramrod was sleeping it off.

'Is he always like this when he's sozzled?'

Turner did not actually answer the question. He said: 'He's a mighty unpredictable cuss: he surprised even me this time.'

'What's Nolly got to say about it?'

'He surprised Nolly, too. But Nolly was drunk. He can't remember what he said. He figures it must've been somep'n pretty bad to effect Matt that way.'

'Has there been bad blood between them before?'

'Not that I know of. Unless Matt's jealous of Nolly and Julia Lakeman.'

'Howzat?' said Tim Greer quickly. He felt a little uncomfortable as both the men gazed at him.

Turner said: 'Nolly goes around a lot with Julia. Maybe Matt has a crush on the gal too. I wouldn't know.'

'Are Nolly and Miss Julia engaged?'

'Well – not officially.'

There were a few more questions Tim would have liked to ask but he let them ride. He did not like the quizzical way the two older men were looking at him. Particularly Nevada and little wonder, for Tim had never posed as a lady-killer before! And, by gosh, he wouldn't now. Why should he bother about Miss Julia Lakeman? First that pantywaist of a sheriff, and now the blonde handsome ranchman! She must be a regular little man-killer!

He fell into step with Nevada and Brad as they walked back towards the ranchhouse. The rancher said: 'I asked Nolly about what Bill Lakeman told us. Nolly has half-changed his mind about selling out. Anyway, Gowans hasn't been near him. Nolly had also thought about bringing gunfighters in – fighting fire with fire he calls it. But he hasn't told anybody except a few of his men. He can't think how Bill Lakeman's got to know about it so soon.'

'Maybe Bill Lakeman's got the same idea and

he's trying to use Nolly as a sort of cover-up,' said Tim.

'They've got a right to bring gunfighters in from outside if they want. Maybe they'll be needed.'

'How about you?'

'My men wouldn't like it. They've all been told they can quit if they want to, but nobody has. I'm gonna depend on them as long as I can.' Brad paused. Then he said: 'Anyway, maybe the Bishop's moved on.' But he did not sound very hopeful.

The partners left the boss and did a bit of riding. When they returned the blood-red setting sun was staining the hills and the range was full of a slumbering peace. A few of the men were already in the mess-hut having early-evening chow. They grunted greetings.

As Nevada and Tim were sitting down the door crashed open and Jarando lurched in. 'Simon,' he bawled. The cook bustled out of the kitchen. 'Bring some chow and plenty of coffee down to my crib.'

'Sure Matt, sure.'

Jarando glared around him and then backed out, slamming the door behind him. Nobody except the cook-boy saw him again that evening. The cook-boy reported him as being in a vile temper.

That night in his bunk Tim Greer found he couldn't sleep. He lay on his back with his hands behind his head. Despite himself he could not evade the vision that rose up in his mind's eye, that became so clear that it was almost like a living presence in the darkness; the vital features of a tawny-haired girl. Maybe he had been a little too hard on her, had surmised things about her. He had no proof that she thought anything at all about the fancy-pants sheriff, except to defend him when he was riled: her sweet nature talking. And why shouldn't she knock around with Nolly Travers, or with anybody else she pleased? Nolly was big and handsome in a washed-out kind of way, maybe the gel was sweet on him. Matt Jarando was a man to be reckoned with, too. Whether you liked the man or not you had to admit he was real salty. Why shouldn't he set his cap at Julia if he wanted to?

Doggone it, the territory was full of handsome ginks. That sheriff – although was no chicken – with his manly figure and fancy clothes and waxed moustachios! Come to think of it, what had happened to Mr Lawman Francis Lord? Tim couldn't remember seeing him around in town today – and everybody else had been there.

Hell, maybe the man had gotten on the trail of the Bishop's Riders and was following 'em plumb into Canada or someplace. Tim Greer punched his pillow viciously, rolled on his side, and tried hard to sleep. But he was not destined to do so. Pretty soon his body was going to be even more active than his mind.

CHAPTER SEVEN

The sound of hoof-beats drumming in the distance made him sit up, instantly alert. The sound came nearer and pretty soon he knew without a doubt that the riders were approaching the ranch.

He felt in the darkness for his trousers. He got into them, then into his boots. Finally he strapped on his gunbelt. He could hear somebody else stirring near him but he was not sure who it was.

The horses clattered into the yard. Then there were running footsteps, and even as Tim crossed the room to the door it was flung open.

'We've caught a couple of the buzzards!' a voice yelled. 'They're out there!'

It was as if a bomb had been dropped in the dark bunkhouse. In an instant there was pandemonium as men tumbled from their bunks. It seemed that very few of them had really been sleeping peacefully. Some of them probably thought they were being attacked. Tim Greer lit the lamp quickly in case of accidents.

'Put out that light!' bawled somebody.

'It's all right, you crazy coots!' yelled Tim. 'It's just a couple of the boys with some news.'

'We've caught a couple of the Bishop's men!' shrilled the man at the door. 'They tried to shoot their way through but we got 'em good!'

The second man came in. 'We'll have a little hanging party,' he bawled. 'Teach the buzzards a lesson!'

Everybody was awake now and getting dressed. It was a savage awakening. Breathing fire and blood, they began to surge towards the door. They streamed across to the corral to get their horses.

Brad Turner came running from the ranch-house, yelling, 'What's going on?' They told him.

He did not hesitate long. 'I guess there's nothing else for it,' he said. 'It's a lesson they want. But we'll do it right. Nobody rides until I'm good an' ready to lead 'em, y' understand? And I want six men to stay here in case anything happens.' He called out names and the disgruntled half-dozen returned to the bunkhouse.

It did not take Turner long to get ready. Pretty soon he returned with his horse and, following the directions of the two men who had brought the news, led the cavalcade out on the range.

There was silence now, except for the thudding of the horses' hoofs. The men, now the full flush of fury had died, had begun to realize what they were going out to do – not in the heat of battle, not madly or gloriously, but in cold blood.

It was a dark night and the inevitable prairie wind sang a dirge to the muffled tom-tom rhythm of the horses' hoofs. The pace became less wild, the men rode steadily. Brad Turner led them purposefully, erect in the saddle.

They approached the mesquite basin ringed by cottonwoods. Down there a light glowed dimly. As they broke through the outer ring of trees a voice shouted:

'Hold it or we'll start shooting!'

'It's all right,' replied one of the guides. 'It's us an' the boss.'

Four men came out of the trees, guns ready. They said 'Howdy', gruffly, and the horsemen went past them. No pleasantries were exchanged. From the other side of the dip came the sound of cattle grazing and bawling.

The light came from a storm-lantern which stood on an old tree stump in among the tangled mesquite, whose bittersweet smell rose on the night air. The standing men were illumined but indistinctly, except for the two strangers, with their hands tied behind them, who stood in the centre of the circle. One was tall, the other short. They looked like a pair of saddle tramps.

The tall one was bareheaded and he looked kind of beat. His head was hanging. The little one wore his hat, but somebody had knocked it over his eyes. He stood erect, defiantly, his little pouter-pigeon chest out-thrust. Maybe it was a little easier for him; he had no noose round his neck as had his tall friend. The rope snaked downwards from the latter's throat and lay coiled at his feet.

'Well, if you're gonna hang 'em at all you'd better give the little one a necktie, too!' said Brad Turner, harshly. 'It's up to you, boss,' said a man quietly.

They had been hanging around too long. They could have done it in the first place, after the strangers were jumped and the tall one, who was faster than he looked, had begun shooting. After they had taken them and roughed them around; they could have done it then. Maybe they would've, only somebody said the rest of the boys ought to know. This was a big thing, this striking back – this lesson! The rest of the boys ought to know!

Since then they had hung around. They had waited – and when men wait they have to think. Also they'd had to listen – to the tall man's expression of his utter contempt for them, uttered coarsely and breathlessly, because he was hurt, and followed by an abysmal silence from which they could not shake him. They had also listened to the little man's calm and lucid explanations of why they were here and where they had come from, and why they should not be legible for the chief roles in a necktie party.

He made it all sound so convincing. But his partner did not join him in his explanations. His attitude said plainer than words that nothing you told these blood-lusting gallow-ghouls would make any difference to the ultimate end.

'They plugged Johnny Peters,' volunteered a *Snake W* man.

From behind the circle Johnny Peters groaned hollowly to substantiate these words. 'F'r Pete's sake!' said somebody, else. 'You'll live!'

The voices were rough with enforced jollity, quavery with tension. 'Let's get it over with,' said one, and Brad Turner said, 'The Riders could sweep down and wipe us all out while we're standing around here.'

'Boss, you don't think—?' The man left the sentence unfinished. Another one came forward and placed a noose around the little man's neck.

Nobody seemed to hear what Nevada Jenkins said or Brad Turner's 'Wait a minute!' 'Over to the cottowoods with them!' shouted somebody.

The lariat merchant was turning, playing out the rope, when the little man kicked him in the backside and he went sprawling into the ring of men. The tall man came alive at the same time and, rushing forward, began kicking out right and left. Yelling men scattered, then closed in, grabbing at them.

It was all so grotesque and rather pitiful. Men closed in, engulfing the fractious pair. The tall one's terrible curses rose to the high heavens, then they were choked off. As the tumult and milling died a little a shot rang out, splitting the night apart. Silence fell swiftly, such a silence as might be expected after the sounding of the last trump.

'I'm sorry, folks,' said Tim Greer. 'I had to do that. Nevada and the boss have both been trying to make themselves heard for the last couple of minutes and nobody's paid 'em any heed. There just ain't no need to get all worked up again. Nobody's gonna string these two men while my pardner an' me are here.'

'Why not?' bawled a man. 'You're horning in again, are you? It's time—'

'Wait a minute!' Brad Turner's voice rose. 'Nevada an' Tim know these ginks. They know they couldn't have been with the Bishop's men the other night.'

'Then why did they start shooting when we came across em?'

The tall stranger spoke up harshly. 'Wouldn't you start shooting if you was attacked by a bunch of rampaging madmen? Here was me an' my pardner getting fixed to settle down for the night—' He broke off as Tim Greer sauntered into the aura of the light. Then he said:

'Hulloa, sport! Don't tell me you're tied up with this mob of loud-mouthed jackals!'

'They're not so bad when you get to know 'em. They made a mistake, that's all.'

'Wal, I'm mighty obliged to yuh for telling me. Imagine that – an' I refused to play with them.'

'I told 'em!' burst in the little man. 'I told 'em—' He suddenly became inarticulate, began to splutter. Tim Greer stepped forward and took the rope from around his neck. 'You're quite a little bobcat when you ain't drunk, aren't you.'

The *Snake W* boys had listened to the cross-talk patter for a few moments in stupified silence. Suddenly one of them spoke up in a semi-choked voice: 'What's the idea? What the—?'

'Tell them, Nevada,' said Tim.

Nevada walked into the circle and told them that the prisoners were the two wranglers Tim and he had met in Pedro's Casino outside Kansas City three days ago. He had told Brad Turner about them when Tim and he first arrived. The boss substantiated this; some of the men remembered the occasion.

Nevada turned to the two men. 'You emptied that barrel finally, huh?'

The tall man jerked his head. 'Yeh, it's lying in a ditch a dozen miles back, empty as a drum.'

There was not much more talking done. The men's bonds were cut and they accompanied Brad, Nevada and Tim and the rest of the boys, together with the wounded Johnny Peters, back to the ranch, leaving the disgruntled nightriders behind to continue with their cattle-nursing.

The two men introduced themselves as 'Lofty' Brown and 'Shorty' Thomas, which seemed almost too good to be true. Inevitably, Brad Turner promised them jobs. They could sleep in the barn until cribs were fitted up for them in the bunkhouse.

'Our thanks to you, boss,' said Lofty sardonically, 'Necks an' all.'

'And no drinking on the job,' added Turner as a stern afterthought.

'Sure, boss.'

So the cavalcade reached the ranch and split up. The boss himself escorted the two new recruits to their sleeping quarters. The rest went to the bunkhouse, where Johnny Peters, who was not badly hurt, was handed over to the ministrations of the cook.

Men began to bed down. There was little talk until somebody asked where was Pete Garner? Then it transpired that nobody could recollect having seen Garner with the riding men. Neither had the half-a-dozen men who had stayed behind to hold the fort seen him, although they confessed that they had only pretended to return to the bunkhouse; they had in reality raided the kitchen for a midnight feed.

'To hell with Garner, anyway!' said a man, and lay down with a huge sigh.

'Maybe we'd better go look outside,' said Nevada Jenkins, and suited the action to the words. His partner followed him. Nobody else seemed over-keen to fall in line. But who could blame the *Snake W* men? Of late they had had their bellyful of fractious strangers.

A shadowy figure came around the corner of the bunkhouse. Both the partners half-reached for their guns. 'It's Brad,' said Nevada.

The boss said: 'That Lofty man is kind of chewed up, though he ain't complaining much. I want

Simon to go an' take a look at him as soon as he's finished with Peters.'

Nevada said: 'We're looking for Pete Garner; he seems to have disappeared.'

'Huh?' said Brad Turner. He waved his arms about aimlessly. He seemed to be working up to a first-rate fit of jitters. 'I'll be with you in a minute,' he said, and made off in the other direction, towards the kitchen.

The two partners went into the darkness. They split up.

Nevada was moving away when Tim hissed warningly.

Nevada turned back. They came together and as one man drew their guns. They skirted the corral. 'I don't hear a thing,' whispered Nevada.

Actually the night was full of sounds, the sighing of the wind through the tall grass, the occasional moaning of cattle in the distance, the instant creaking of a rickety fence, a murmur of voices from back in the bunkhouse. It was a jumble of tiny sounds which seemed somehow only a part of the general stillness.

Then suddenly there was a noise which was unmistakably that of stumbling footsteps. Instinctively both men went down on their haunches and crouched against the corral fence. The footsteps stopped.

'Show yourself, whoever you are,' said Tim softly, 'or we'll start shooting.'

'It's me, boys!' cried a familiar voice.

Pete Garner came out of the shadows with a rush. He lurched and almost fell. He held on to the top rail of the corral fence. 'Oh, my head!' he said.

The two men reached him. As they did so they heard footsteps and turned. Brad Turner came out of the darkness. Just then the bunkhouse door opened, letting out a stream of light. Figures passed across this stream, half-obscuring it. There were more footsteps.

'Here we go again,' said Tim Greer softly. 'What fine targets those crazy jackasses make!'

As if he had received a telepathic communication from the young man, Brad Turner called out, 'Douse that damn light!' As he joined the three men by the corral fence the light went out.

Pete Garner said quickly, 'I was a bit late coming out of the bunkhouse when you all went a-riding. If you remember, I put my horse in the little toolshed because there wasn't room for him in the stables. He's a cantankerous little cuss; but the time I'd got him out you were on the trail. I was about to follow when I thought I heard somep'n moving out there.' He pointed to a spot in the vicinity of Matt Jarando's cabin. 'I went across to investigate. There's a lot of mesquite there. The skunk must've jumped me from behind one o' them clumps. He suttinly gave me an almighty wallop. I only just came round.' Garner felt gingerly in his hair.

More men came along, voluble in their questioning. Brad Turner shut them up. 'Give a hand,' he said harshly.

'Matt Jarando!' cried Tim Greer suddenly, and turned and streaked away. Nevada followed him.

Tim reached the little cabin. His skin prickled as he gazed into the darkness all round him. Nevada joined him.

The door was unlocked. Tim opened it and they went inside. The place was in pitch darkness except for the faint square of light which was the half-curtained window. There was a smell of stale air and whisky.

'The light,' said Tim hoarsely. 'Goldarnit! Where's the light?'

He groped around and almost knocked a table over. 'Matt!' he said. 'Matt!'

His fingers touched the cold glass of the lamp on the table. As he reached for matches his hands trembled. He was trying to listen, too, but all he could hear was the thumping of his own heart. After what seemed centuries, he struck a match and lit the lamp.

The room sprang into garish relief. Nevada closed the door with a little thud. They looked around the room. Finally their eyes became focussed on the bunk beneath the window.

Matt Jarando lay on his back with his mouth wide open. He was fully dressed except for his boots; just the way they had left him. One of his arms hung down beside the bunk, the other was thrown across his throat.

They went closer to him. His chest rose and fell. A strange rasping noise, midway between a snore and a sigh, came from his throat. He stank of rotgut red-eye. But he looked as vital and alive as a slumbering panther.

The partners exchanged glances. Tim expelled a gust of breath. He said:

'Well, the midnight prowler wasn't after *him*, it seems – or, if he was, Pete scared him away.'

CHAPTER EIGHT

A search was made that night but no clues were found. And it seemed no place had been broken into, and, as far as could be ascertained, nothing had been taken.

By morning light no more signs had been discovered. Matt Jarando was surprised to learn of the rumpus that had been going on while he was in dreamland. When he heard of Pete Garner's accident he enquired solicitously of the latter's condition. So it seemed the rift in the lute was bridged for the time being. However, Matt was not so tractable when he learned that while he slept a couple more characters had been added to his circus.

He went back to his cabin to sulk. He had his breakfast there, too.

Another character who was not present at the bunkhouse for chow was Pete Garner who was sleeping off the headache caused by the egg-shaped lump on his head.

Bunks had been made ready for Lofty Brown

and Shorty Thomas and after breakfast they went along to the bunkhouse to view their new home. As they entered with the rest of the men Pete Garner was rising. Nevada asked him how he felt and he said he'd be all right once he had had a meal. The two new men stood in the middle of the bunkhouse and stared at the man with the white bandage around his head.

Lofty said suddenly, 'Pete Lagrue!'

The other's head jerked up. His eyes focused on Lofty.

'Are you speaking to me?' he said softly.

'Yes. I called you by name that was all.'

The man who called himself Pete Garner moved a little closer to Lofty. His eyes were frosty. He seemed about to speak again but it was Tim Greer who beat him to it.

'He's right isn't he? You *are* Pete Lagrue.'

Garner turned his head. 'What makes you think that, Tim?' he asked almost mildly.

'I don't *think*; I'm sure. I saw that scar on your back when you were at the pumps. From the first I knew there was something familiar about you, and, after that, I was sure. I saw you get that scar – it was in Abilene wasn't it?'

Pete Garner turned about, walked back to his bunk, sat down almost wearily. Only then did he speak.

'Go on,' he said.

'All right – I was only a kid but I remember it well. You weren't so very old yourself. You got said. 'But there is one thing I'd like to know; does Brad Turner know who you are?'

'Yeh, he knows.'

There was a stir. A loud voice said, 'I don't believe that.'

'Why'n't you ask him?' drawled Pete.

'I will.' The door slammed. The man could be heard hurrying away.

Pete Garner rose to his feet. 'Don't let it throw you, boys,' he said. He crossed the room, passing through them. He went out of the door, closing it gently behind him. A few seconds later he was heard splashing around the pumps.

The loudmouthed man came back looking a little crestfallen. 'Well?' said Nevada Jenkins and the man looked at him sullenly. 'The boss told me to mind my own business, he knew who Lagrue was all along. It was Lagrue's wish that he call himself Garner, so Turner let him be.'

'So the galoot is ashamed of his name.'

'On the contrary, pardner.' Lagrue stood in the doorway. 'I just didn't want to wound the gentle susceptibilities of you people. Would anybody like to call me a liar?'

The man leaned negligently against the door-jamb. He was unarmed. But nobody took him up. Nobody spoke at all in fact until Tim Greer said; 'Let's take Mr Lagrue as we find him, shall we? Unless he'd like any other way.' There was no hint of backing-down in the young man's tone. He faced the famous gunman, unblinkingly, his thumbs mixed up in a brawl in the International, you caught one of the gamblers cheating or something and you beat him up. The boss of the International, Croner, set his boys on to you. They disarmed you and stripped you to the waist in the middle of Texas Street. Then Croner, who used to be an overseer down South before he moved this way, brought out his whip. He would have beaten you to death if other folks hadn't intervened. They said you'd be scarred for life. You left town but a couple of nights later you came back. You killed Croner, killed him fair in a gun-battle.'

Tim's voice died away. For a moment Garner did not speak. He sat looking into space and all hell was in his eyes, then he said gently, 'Do you know Tim, that was the first time I'd killed a man? I was just a kid.'

His voice died and for a moment there was dead silence as everybody watched him. Then a voice somewhere by the door said softly, 'Pete Lagrue, the Texas killer.'

Even then the man did not move or speak. Lofty Brown said: 'I recognized you right away. And my pardner did. You came from the same part of the country as us. I didn't know but what the folks here knew who you were. Maybe I ought to've kept my big mouth shut. I've got nothing against Pete Lagrue.'

'Thanks, friend,' said Pete. Then he looked at Tim Greer. 'Why didn't you tell everybody?'

The young man's lip curled. 'Why should I?' he

hooked in his belt. Lagrue smiled a little and said 'I'm in your hands, boys.'

'The man never done me any harm,' said Lofty Brown suddenly and his little pardner backed him up with a loud 'Aye' which might have meant anything. Lagrue moved away from the doorway and men dissolved before him. 'Thanks, boys,' he said, smiling again.

Tim Greer watched him, admiring the coolness of the man. He had to admit to himself that there was something he liked about Lagrue, something inherent in the man which awakened an echo in himself.

Everybody started as Matt Jarando came in. He was his peevish self once more. 'The party's over,' he said. Something, maybe the atmosphere, puzzled him, but he made no comment. He looked at Lagrue and said; 'The boss says you can stay put if you don't feel like riding.'

'I'm all right. I'll go along with the rest.' He smiled thinly again and Jarando looked at him curiously, looked as if he was going to say more but didn't. Tim Greer wondered if the foreman knew of Pete Garner's real identity and if that was the reason of his sudden change of front towards the man. Much as he disliked Jarando, however, he did not think he was the sort to kow-tow to anybody, gunman or not, for fear of his own skin. Jarando had a fast rep: maybe he thought he could out shoot the fabulous Pete Lagrue if occasion arose.

The foreman whirled in his tracks. 'Don't stand

around like a lot of dummies,' he bawled. 'Get your stuff.'

The men got their gear together and followed him outside. He gave out the orders. As men began to split up into bunches and move away he said 'Wait a minute.' Then he looked again at the man called Pete who was mounted, his sombrero perched atop of a cocoon of bandages giving him a rather incongruous appearance.

'You know this man's real name: Pete Lagrue?' It was half-question half statement.

'We know, Matt.'

'Maybe he wouldn't mind if we call him by his proper name.'

'He won't mind,' said the man in question cooly. 'He hopes it won't get the ranch a bad name.'

'It won't – if nobody outside knows of it.' Jarando's glance swept the men. His meaning was plain.

Nobody said anything. The horsemen filtered away to get on with their appointed tasks. Lagrue, silent now, went with Tim and Nevada and three other men. Their job was to round up strays and – they all knew it although they hadn't been told – scout for signs.

The range was quiet, too quiet; everybody was on tenterhooks, everybody wondered what the other side was doing and when the next blow would fall. Everybody was suspicious of his neighbour. The three old *Snake W* hands rode a little apart from the three strangers. Nobody said much.

Lagrue was unusually silent. Nevada was his usual self; even Tim Greer never knew what went on behind the seamed face with the ironically-puckered lips and grin-wrinkled eyes. For himself, his thoughts were buzzing round inside his head like a bee in a barrel.

Why had Brad Turner, who had been indignant at the thought of other men bringing strange gunnies into the valley, hired one himself; and one of the worst in the West at that. Hired him secretly too and under another name. What was this lean man with the bleak blue eyes, Lagrue, thinking as he rode along. Why exactly was he here? – surely not as a common cowhand. What had this man from the lawless ranges of the Pecos to do with Trinity Valley. And, what was more important still, what had his presence to do with the Bishop's Riders?

He wondered also whether Matt Jarando had known the man's identity all along or whether somebody had only just slipped him the word.

In the scrubland around the edges of the valley and at the bases of the hills were small farms inhabited by those people known the length and breadth of the West as 'nesters'. In many parts of the cattle-lands they would have long since been driven away. But the ranchers of Trinity Valley were, in the main, pretty tolerant people – and, anyway, the scrubland was of little use to them – so they let the nesters stay, always keeping a weather eye on them, however, to see that they did not attempt to encroach on other people's preserves.

The nesters of Trinity Valley were a tractable lot. If they heard of the bloody range wars which were going on in Texas and other parts of the cattle-country, battles for land in which nesters were slaughtered by men of the big ranches and *vice-versa*, it had no effect on them. They were, it seemed, content to live at peace with their more powerful neighbours and sell them eggs and vegetables, and even do odd jobs for them, and ride for them at round-up time.

The way of life in Trinity Valley was an ideal thing and the quota of nesters grew; and though a few of the smaller ranchers looked askance at their numbers, their doubts were pretty soon put to rest, for the nesters seemed to spend more time squabbling among themselves over bits of land than irritating their more prosperous neighbours.

The nesters were mostly half-breeds, Mexicans, Indians and shanty Irish from back East. They were a quarrelsome crowd but a jolly crowd, too, fond of kissing and making-up, and having wild parties in the hills. The Irish, particularly, liked fighting for fighting's sake. They were a shiftless lot with no great love of money and land and possessions, but, on the whole, were pretty decent people. They were shocked at the depradations of the Bishop's Riders but figured, quite rationally, that the murdering rustlers would not bother with such as they. But they were mistaken it seemed, and Jules

Gaynor was the first to find this out.

Jules had the farm near the mouth of the Widow Pass. He was a 'breed,' but of what particular mixtures nobody was certain. He was a wizened taciturn fellow with long hair like an Indian and black sloe eyes. He had a fat wife and a brood of children. People were never quite sure how many children Jules really had. The place always seemed to be swarming with them, the reason being that all the nesters' kids used Jules' place and the rocks behind it as a playground. Actually Jules had four of his own but he was very fond of kids and did not mind how many used his place as a battleground. When night fell, however, all the alien breed, the Irish, the Mexican and the rest were sent off home and Jules basked in the warmth of his own little family circle.

It was one of many nights so similar when he sat in his armchair sucking at his pipe, his wife sitting opposite him and the three youngest kids playing on the hearth that Jules received his visitors. The eldest boy, sixteen-year-old Tony, as dark and wizened and taciturn as his father, was out riding. The two old people heard him returning; he was riding fast.

'That boy!' said Mamma. 'He is wild – he will break his neck.'

'He is wild, yes,' said Jules. 'But, never fear, he is a good horseman.'

A few seconds later the door burst open and Tony came in. He stood shielding his eyes from the light, with a brown hand. 'There's a big bunch of riders coming this way,' he said.

'So,' said Jules and took his pipe from his mouth. 'Sit down, boy, there is some coffee for you.'

Tony sat down, his sloe eyes darting restlessly around the room. His mother rose and with a sidelong glance at her husband went over to the stove. The sound of drumming hoofs came nearer and nearer.

At first the people in the house had thought the riders were making for the pass. But now as they listened and the hoofbeats rose to a crescendo it became evident that the riders were coming to the farm.

'Jules, what is it?' Mrs Gaynor looked up from the stove.

'It is probably some of Mr Turner's or Mr Lakeman's riders coming to pay us a call. Get the boy his coffee.'

'It sounds too many for that,' said young Tony. Mechanically he took the cup from his mother.

The horses halted outside. There was a clattering of hoofs on hard ground and a jingling of harness, but only one voice seemed to be speaking. The three smaller children, two girls and a boy, had risen from the hearth, where they had been playing their childish version of the old Indian game of 'bones'.

'Let's go an' see the men, poppa,' said seven-year-old Al.

Jules rose. 'No, you stay here, I will go. Maybe I will bring a few of our visitors to see you.' He rose and made for the door.

'Take your gun, pop,' said Tony.

'Gun? Why for a gun to greet visitors?' Jules opened the door and stepped outside. He left the door slightly ajar.

There was no more sound for a bit except the noise of restless horses and jingling harness. Then Jules' voice rose.

'Hey, who are you? What do you want? What you doing with that torch? I don't—'

The rest of his sentence was never uttered – or it was drowned by a shot. Then came another shot; and another.

Tony sprang to his feet. Then he stood, white-faced. Everybody else in the room was transfixed. There were stumbling footsteps, like those of a very old man trying to run, then the door swung open. Jules staggered in, his arms outstretched, a terrible look on his face.

His hands were outstretched towards his wife. 'Dolores,' he croaked. 'Dolores. They—'

As she ran towards him he fell on his face. She went down on her knees before him and, mutely, tried to turn him over. Tony ran to her side and helped her. The dead face looked up at them. Tony rose to his feet, crossed the room and took the rifle from the pegs over the fireplace. He checked it and found it fully loaded.

He retraced his steps, passing the body of his

father where his mother knelt like a craven image. The three children began to follow him, the two girls whimpering a little. He shut the door and dropped the bar into place. He turned and said, 'Get back there. Get back I tell you!'

They backed before this changed Tony, sensing in him now the authority which had been their father's, half-understanding why it should be so.

Tony held the curtain aside and looked out. When he turned his head fear flickered in his eyes. It was a fear of something he could not understand.

'The Bishop's Riders!' he cried. 'They're setting the barn on fire.' For a moment of time he hesitated, grief and rage fighting with the superstitions handed down to him from ancient ancestors.

Then he said, 'I'll want some more shells, momma,' and he saw his mother rise and he knew that she too had come out of her stupor, that she too was ready to fight. She made the whimpering children get down behind the huge overstuffed armchair in the corner, then she climbed on to a stool and reached into the cupboard for the shells.

The riders were doing their work thoroughly. As far as they were concerned, resistance – such as it had been, an old greaser without a gun, shot down like the dog they believed him to be – was at an end. They made no reckoning of the women and kids. What good was a fat old greaser woman to them. The scum could get out the back way and run, or they could stay and be burnt alive in their own house. It was all the same to the Riders.

Yes, they figured they had nothing more to worry about at this tumbledown farm. Consequently they were almighty surprised when young Tony started shooting. The youngster had been a hunter almost ever since he could walk, he had eyes like a mountain-cat, and a steady trigger-finger to boot. Two of the Riders, etched grotesquely against the leaping flames, crumpled earthwards to die. Another man cried out with pain and, clutching his shoulder, staggered away from the light. The hooded leader gave the order to take cover.

CHAPTER NINE

The Riders moved away from the aura of the flickering fire-glow and took cover among the miscellaneous junk with which the Gaynor yard was littered. Tony's shots became wildly spaced; they had a searching quality. Then the Riders, after spotting his position, opened up. Tony left the window at which he crouched and dodged across to the next. As he passed the door a slug whipped through its upper part and sang over his head. The door was flimsy, the timbers rotten.

'Get in cover, momma!' he shouted. 'Get with the kids.'

But she kept making her journeys to and from the cupboard until all the shells they possessed were at Tony's side. She helped him drag furniture against the front and back doors.

'There's nothing more you can do now, momma,' he said. 'Go back. Go back.'

She went and sat in the corner with her children, enfolded them in her arms, held them against her ample bosom. With black fatalistic eyes she watched her son. He fired at flashes out there, the barn was now merely a smouldering heap, the rest was blackness. The flashes became mere frequent, they came nearer, they spread out at the side. Slugs came through the walls and windows of the old cabin and zipped across the room. Tony entrenched himself at the window. He knew now there was nothing else he could do. He fired coolly; something inside of him seemed to tell him when he had hit a target. But he didn't hit many now, for the bandits were using all the cover the yard afforded.

The Gaynors were very untidy people. If a wagon-wheel broke it was left where it rolled, side by side with a barrel with a hole in it, a broken trace. They shrugged; 'tomorrow' they said.

Now tomorrow had come and Jules Gaynor lay untidily in his own blood on the floor of his own living-room while his sixteen-year-old son fought for the lives of the mother and the children.

A slug creased Tony's shoulder and he bit off an involuntary cry of pain. He turned savagely. He shouted. 'The back way, momma! Take the kids the back way while you still have time.'

She shook her head mutely, her dark eyes wide. He sprang to his feet. 'The kids, momma!' he screamed. 'The kids.' The window smashed behind him and he clapped his hand to his cheek. She saw the blood spurt through his fingers. He went down to his knees. He waved the blood-stained hand. 'Go!' he screamed. 'Go!' The children began to scream at the sight of his bleeding face. Mrs Gaynor rose and almost enveloped them in her ample skirts as she guided them towards the back door. 'Hurry, momma,' she heard Tony shout 'Hurry.'

She moved a couple of chairs aside, lifted the bar, opened the door, pushed the children out into the darkness. 'Run.' She said, 'Run.' She turned to go back to her son. The two men came out of the blackness so swiftly that they were upon her before she could cry out. A big hand was clapped over her mouth and she was dragged outside. She heard the other man say, 'Set 'em on the trail.'

The man who held her said gruffly, 'Maybe the Bishop—'

'Do as I say!'

She felt herself being dragged along. The children were running in front of her as the man shouted. She knew the other man had gone into the house. She wanted to cry out, to warn Tony, but the brutal hand at her mouth prevented her from doing so.

When Tony turned, the second man was inside the room. Tony ducked and the first shot went over his head. Crouching, his rifle at hip-level he fired and saw the man stagger. Then a terrible blow in his shoulder spun him half-round and he caught hold of the window ledge to steady himself. He felt another slug go past his ear; the man stood in the doorway but he was swaying. The rifle had gone suddenly very heavy but Tony managed to lift it and squeeze the trigger, at the same time he was rising, going forward, and the man was crumpling, a little indistinct. Then the man was still. To get through the door Tony had to climb over him. It was the hardest thing he had ever done. His legs felt like ton-weights and so did the rifle. His shoulder felt like it was broken, the blood was seeping from it; it was dragging him down.

He went out through the door into the darkness and he fired at the flashes all around him. The blows hit him from all sides, tearing at first, then numbing, paralysing, until he could not hold the rifle any more and he felt it fall. He sank, his fingers scrabbling at the ground. His father's ground, *his* ground. And there he died.

The Bishop said let the woman and the children go, they would have a tale to tell. The riders set fire to the rest of the Gaynor homestead and, leaving it blazing to the skies behind them swept on.

The next homestead belonged to Pat Mahoney who lived there with his beautiful young half-caste wife, Lolita. There was just the two of them; they had not been married long.

Nevada, Tim, Lagrue and the three other *Snake W* men were returning from their scouting trip and coming through the hills when they saw the glow in the sky. They urged their mounts forward and reached the crest of the rise and looked down. The blaze was over to the right of them; already it seemed to be dying. One of the men gave an exclamation and pointed. Almost directly below them, though far below, another fire was beginning. As they watched tongues of flame leaped up suddenly, like living snakes, reaching for the high heavens. As one man they urged their horses down the perilous slopes, risking their necks in their urgency.

They were almost on the level when they thought they heard the sound of galloping hoofs, going away on the night winds. But they saw nothing. Their guns were out as they approached the dying fire. The horses began to shy so the men dismounted on the last lap and went forward on foot. Lagrue was in front. He stopped suddenly in his tracks crying, 'God, what's that?'

A white figure was silhouetted against the ruddy glow. Then it began to run. Lagrue started forward. Then, a little clumsily in his riding-boots, began to run too.

Tim Greer was close behind him. Lagrue was almost on the figure when it turned and began to scream. The sound made Tim's blood run cold. He saw Lagrue's back stiffen; the man's steps flagged. The figure began to run again, still screaming and waving its arms above its head. Tim realized then that it was a woman.

She swung around again as Lagrue overtook her. She flung up her hands and, still screaming, fell on her back. The scream sounded like words now, words in an incoherent string, pleading words in a jumble of Spanish and broken English.

Lagrue was bending over her, trying to soothe her. Tim reached them and went down on one knee. The dying fire bathed the scene in a red glow which seemed terribly symbolic of blood and violence. The woman was almost naked. All she wore were her underclothes, and they were in tatters. She was young and dark and beautiful, but her eyes were demented as she cowered before the two men. He saw that her flesh, rosy in the firelight, was bruised and scratched in dozens of places.

'We're not going to hurt you,' said Lagrue softly. 'W're your friends.'

Tim was surprised at the utter gentleness of the man's voice. A strange voice, it was, as if somebody else, somebody gentle and kind, was speaking through the bitter lips of the lean killer. The man's hand moved upwards to brush the woman's hair from her eyes. She screamed again, and both men involuntarily recoiled a little.

Nevada and two other men came up. One of the men gabbled. 'That's Mrs Mahoney! The Bishop done it – it must've been the Bishop!' His eyes shone horridly and redly in the light as he looked around him fearfully.

'She thinks we belong to that mob,' said Tim. He was speaking half to himself; he was beside himself. His heart was sick with horror and loathing for the men who had done such things to this beautiful creature; he wanted to do something, but he didn't know what to do. He leaned nearer, mouthing soothingly but not knowing what he was saying. He reached out to touch her and she began to scream again.

'For God's sake!' said one of the men.

The last member of the party ran up. 'I found Pat Mahoney,' he said. 'He's burned up a lot. He was dead even before the fire caught him, though, I guess – full of holes.' He broke off. 'Can't you stop her? Can't you—'

He sighed as the woman ceased to scream. But she continued to make those horrible little pleading noises. Old Nevada had moved away. He returned with the horses. 'There's nothing we can do here,' he said, 'except to get this poor girl away from the scene as quickly as possible. That might save her life and her reason.' There was an age-old weariness in his voice. In his younger days he had fought Indians; he had seen what they could do to the squaws of the hated palefaces who drove them from their hunting grounds. But this was no Indian work, and there had been no reason for it, either. That last was the hardest thought to bear.

He bent over the girl and talked to her, and after a while she became silent. Maybe her demented eyes saw in his old face something that had not been in those of the younger men. She let Nevada lift her and place her on his horse. Lagrue spoke up: 'Will you and Tim take her in while me an' the boys go an' investigate that other blaze?'

This was agreed upon, so the partners set off.

The girl was very still against the old man's breast. Her eyes were closed. 'She's hardly breathing,' said Nevada.

They were met by a bunch of the boys who had been starting out to investigate the glow in the sky. Two of them retraced their steps, galloping as couriers before the partners and their burden. The rest went on to join Lagrue and the rest. Maybe they would be able to exact vengeance on somebody for this night, but Tim Greer had a terrible fear that they would be too late, that they were already too late.

Brad Turner was awaiting them when they got back to the ranch. He led them upstairs to where a bed was already made. 'One of the boys has ridden to Bancoville for Doc Larney,' be said. When they laid the girl on the bed she was in a coma and there was a white froth at her lips.

'We ought to have a woman here, too,' said old Nevada. Then he checked himself from saying more, remembering Brad's wife, who had died so young and the way Brad hadn't had a woman in his house since.

But Brad's face had not changed, and as his old friend replied Nevada remembered the woman who was always welcome here, where he had met her once himself. 'I'll go,' said Tim quickly. 'All right,' said Brad and the young man ran out. They heard him mount his horse and go galloping away. He was challenged outside the *Circle U* ranch. He was trying to explain himself to two truculent cowhands with drawn guns when Bill Lakeman came on to the scene. Quickly Tim explained his business. The old man was not easily shocked. He led the way and a couple of minutes later he was talking to his daughter. He told her the brief tragic tale himself. She gasped with horror, her hand flying to her mouth. Then she was her normal self again. 'You'd better stay here, dad,' she said. 'I'll be all right with Mr Greer.'

Bill Lakeman argued, but finally the girl had her way. She said he could not spare any men; the ranch should not go unguarded. Also, as he was the boss, his place was right here. The man and the girl started off together. Yes, Miss Julia doubtless thought she'd had her own way, but Tim had a sneaking idea that they were being tracked by a small bunch of *Circle U* men, just in case.

Reaching the *Snake W*, they ran into a harrowing scene. Two of the men who had been with Lagrue had just brought in the bodies of Pat Mahoney and Tony Gaynor. They had left the charred remains of old Jules where they lay, and Lagrue and another man were still scouting after the woman and the kids.

The two men were full of the way the sixteen-year-old Tony must have fought – the way he had been shot to ribbons. 'We found one body we figured belonged to the other side. He must've been shot just inside the door. The fire got him; he's unrecognizable. But the kid must have gotten more than one. There's blood all over the place.

They must've taken their dead an' wounded with 'em.'

Tim saw that the girl's eyes were turned away from the pitiful remains. He admired her composure. However, he could not help wishing he had ridden with her under different circumstances than these. He led her upstairs. The doctor was already there.

CHAPTER TEN

In the early morning Lagrue and the other man brought in Mrs Gaynor and the kids. But they had not seen or heard anything else; they had found nothing.

The man who rode into Bancoville for the doc had called at the sheriff's office, too, and asked for a posse. The posse arrived, led by Sheriff Lord's deputy, Cal Stevens. But there was no sign of the boss lawman. Cal said that he'd ridden out early yesterday morning and had not returned. No, Cal did not know where he had been bound for; the sheriff being a mighty secretive cuss, did not tell him anything.

The posse rampaged over the range and found nothing. The Riders once more seemed to have vanished into the ground. And still there was no sign of Sheriff Francis Lord.

Early the next morning the main ranchers gathered in Brad Turner's living-room. Besides Brad, there was Nolly Travers, Bill Lakeman, Matt Jarando. Also Pete Parsons, Nolly's foreman, Bill's right-hand 'man', his daughter, Julia, Nevada Jenkins, Tim Greer and Pete Lagrue. The rest of the company looked a little askance at the latter, but he was quite at ease and Brad Turner did not seem to see anything strange in his presence there. Tim Greer wondered again why, after being so fiercely indignant about anyone else using outside gunmen, he had taken the step of hiring one himself, and was even admitting him to his counsel. Had Lagrue anything to tell them, he wondered.

His eyes caught Julia's soft gaze and he forgot his questions and smiled. She smiled back; they were pals. She had been up most of the night seeing to Mrs Gaynor and the kids and Lolita Mahoney. Lolita was still in a kind of coma; the doc said he couldn't know how she would be until she came out of it.

Tim marvelled at the girl, looking so fresh and untroubled as she took her place among these harsh men. He realized that he was thinking of her, admiring her, rather more than was good for him. No other woman – he hadn't had a lot of truck with them, in fact – had affected him quite in the way this one did. He was jerked back into reality. Things were getting under way; Bill Lakeman was saying: 'Why did they attack the nesters? What did they expect to get there? And why only two homesteads, anyway? They could've wiped the lot out in a night the way they were going.' Bill, it seemed, although he tolerated the nesters the same as the rest, had little sympathy with them.

Lagrue said: 'Maybe we scared the Riders off too soon – maybe that's what they intended to do – wipe them all out.'

'Humph! But why?'

'Maybe they think the nesters would join up with us, so they've given them a terrible warning, just in case. Maybe it's just the first step in a reign of terror they're planning – just like the old days, the old Bishop's Riders.'

'What do you know about the old days?' said Nolly Travers.

'The Bishop's Riders are a legend. A man can't come near this territory without hearing about them. You hear it most from half-breeds and suchlike. It's on their superstitious natures that these new Riders are playing now. An' some of the cowhands are almost as bad – some of them are already getting the jitters: you could see it going on around you last night.'

'You could, huh—?'

'We won't argue about that right now,' broke in Brad Turner quickly.

'The man's right, anyway,' said Nolly. 'Many of the cowhands, born and bred in the valley and told bogy-tales when they were kids, are full of superstitious fear. It mightn't take much more of this to start a wholesale exodus. I tell you straight, gentlemen, I'm for bringing gunmen in from outside—'

'Wait a minute,' said Bill Lakeman. 'We don't want a range-war. I've been thinking again – I've been thinking hard. Might not it be the nesters who are behind all this? I've never trusted some of those buzzards.'

'But, Bill—'

Lakeman went on, unheeding, 'Isn't it strange that the two nesters who were slaughtered are the two who were most friendly towards us ranchers? Maybe they were killed so they won't talk, maybe the nesters have a scheme to drive us out of the valley and take it over for themselves. They're all foreigners remember; they've heard the legend of the Bishop's Riders and some smart egg among them figured they'd resurrect the Bishop – and his men – for their own ends.'

'Oh, father,' broke in Julia. 'That's unjust – you haven't an atom of proof.'

Watching her, Tim Greer remembered the way she had defended the sheriff, at an earlier date. Her attitude now was the same; she had a very well-developed sense of the rightness of things.

'Just a theory, my dear,' said her father. 'I'd sooner suspect the nesters than suspect my own neighbours.' He looked around him, from face to face, and his meaning was plain. They also understood now what he had meant by his reference to a range war.

Brad Turner broke the rather strained silence, saying, 'What about those Ace people? I figure they might have something to do with it.'

'I don't think so,' said Nolly Travers. 'They seem to have lost all interest in us.'

A voice outside shouted 'Boss!' Brad Turner excused himself and went out. He returned a few seconds later and said: 'That was one of my men just returned from town. He says there is still no sign of Sheriff Lord.'

Dead silence greeted this pronouncement. It seemed unthinkable, although they despised the sheriff as a panty-waist, that he should be mixed up with the Riders, but that was the way things were beginning to point. Why had the sheriff ridden out alone? If he was on the trail of anything, surely he would have taken men with him? – Or was he just a skunk running out while the going was good?

A few seconds later the meeting broke up. Nevada and Tim rode out with Lagrue. As they took the trail the *Circle U* buckboard rattled past them. Julia waved gaily to them but her father sat hunched hugely on his seat and did not even look in their direction.

'A queer cuss that old one,' said Lagrue softly.

The work of the range went on as usual – but men were irritable and jumpy and they did not ride too far out to look for strays. The three newcomers traversed the territory across the Widow Pass; blackened ash, cartridge shells and bloodstained grass told them nothing. They met Lofty Brown and Shorty Thomas, who joined up with them. The two wranglers, their proper job shelved, had another to do which entailed messing with fence-posts and barbed wire, a job any cowhand hated. They enlisted the trio's aid.

The work of the range went on but the evil was in the air, beneath the surface, and all around. It would always be there until the cause of it was removed. Men moved in a fog of mystery and evil, forgetting the sun, watching their neighbours, thinking, thinking – fearing.

Darkness came again. That night Brad Turner had insisted that Tim and Nevada get some rest. Tim was restless however. He left Nevada in the bunkhouse playing poker with a couple of the boys and went outside for a smoke.

He was moving towards the corral when he saw a movement by the corner of the ranchhouse. He dropped his cigarette swiftly and ground it beneath his heel. He retraced his steps and moved into the shadows beside the bunkhouse. He heard soft footsteps coming towards him. He drew his gun. The figure went past him, moving fast but cautiously. He stepped out of the shadows and drove the gun into the nocturnal prowler's back.

'Raise your hands,' he snarled. 'Then freeze.'

The figure gave a little sob of pain. It startled Tim; he realized his gun-barrel was digging into soft flesh and he drew it away.

'Who's that?' said a feminine voice and his worst fears were realized.

'Miss Julia,' he gasped. 'I didn't think it was you. I thought—'

'Tim Greer,' she said. 'Did you throw down on me?'

He could not tell by her voice whether she was angry or not. 'Huh, well yes. I'm almighty sorry. I didn't see you properly – I thought you'd gone home. I thought it was a prowler. I guess we're all kinda jumpy.'

'I didn't figure you for the jumpy type,' she said. 'I guess I asked for it creeping around like this. I didn't want to disturb anybody.' She had turned towards him and now he could see the pale oval of her face. He mumbled something about hurting her but she was still talking so, involuntarily, he put his arm around her back where the gun had been. She did not seem to notice the caressing hand as she went on talking—'Lolita has come round. She remembers everything – I think she's going to be all right. I was just going to the cookhouse to get her something to eat and drink. Maybe she'll be able to talk later on—'

'That's good,' said Tim, 'good,'

She said gently, 'You didn't hurt me very much, Mr Greer, you can take your hand away now. I'll get on.'

He dropped his hand, she began to move away into the darkness. 'I'll come with you,' he said. 'I don't want anybody to make the same mistake as I did.' He started forward and fell into step beside her.

'That's very kind of you, Mr Greer.'

'I wish you'd call me Tim.'

'All right, Tim. Now I'll have to ask you to call

me Julia.' There was a bubbling laughter in her voice.

'If you don't mind.'

'I don't mind – You're the first man who's taken me for a prowler.'

'I'm sorry, Julia.' They laughed softly together, creeping behind the bunkhouse like a pair of conspirators. It was not until they reached the cookhouse door that Tim realized he was holding her hand.

Simon the cook was on the point of retiring but with alacrity he came fully awake and did as the lady ordered, but not without a wry glance at the watchful Tim. When everything was ready on a tray, Tim carried it, and escorted Julia back to the ranchhouse. In the shadow of the veranda he handed the tray to her. She held it in both hands and looked up at him. He saw her smile. 'Thanks, cowboy,' she said. He bent and kissed her.

He held her lightly by the shoulders then he let her go and she was still looking up at him. The pale blob of her face was enigmatic.

'Would you kick a man while he's down, Tim Greer?' she said and he knew she was not mad.

'No, but I'd kiss a woman with a child in her arms,' he quipped. He reached for her again but she twisted away from him and ran nimbly up the veranda steps. He thought he heard a chuckle.

He stood in the darkness grinning until the frame door had closed and he could hear her footsteps no more, then he went back to the bunkhouse. The poker school was still going strong. He went across to his bunk, sat down, got out the makings and rolled himself a smoke. Suddenly, for no reason at all, he began to get peeved. He was not sure what she had meant tonight, not sure of the way she wanted it to be, he was not even sure of his own intentions and it peeved him because he doubted himself and doubted her too. He wondered whether he ought to have offered to take her home after she was finished here. But he knew that her father would be calling for her. He had an idea that Bill Lakeman would not look kindly on Tim's continued association with his daughter. For what was Tim Greer? Just a saddle tramp really, and he probably would never amount to anything else. And hadn't the girl got ranch owner Nolly Travers setting his cap at her? And maybe Matt Jarando too, who was, at least, a straw-boss.

He smoked a couple of cigarettes. Then, as the card-school broke up and everybody made for their bunks, he rolled over and tried to sleep. But he could not sleep, even after the light was doused he could not sleep. That was the reason he heard the shots and was the first out when the echoes of them had died away.

Brad Turner sat on the edge of his bed and stared into space. His mind was full of worries, he was like a man suspended in a void full of mysterious faces whose yammering lips threw questions at him. He was in a daze, he was not aware that he sat, but he could not sleep. Bill Lakeman and his daughter had long since gone and poor Lolita was silent. She had been able to tell them little before she lapsed into that half-coma, again.

How long he sat there while the questions buzzed in his brain Brad did not know, but finally he rose mechanically and began to undress. He looked around the familiar room as if he had never seen it before. But it gave him no comfort. He tried to recapture some memory of the happy times he had spent in this room but he could not manage to do so. It was so long ago, so very long ago. What was this ranch to him, this valley? At this moment he felt just like giving up. What he would do if he gave up he could not think right now. Sell up, maybe, go away. Of what use was it to fight if bad luck beat you in the end? – As it had beaten him before and seemed to be beating him now. Peace in his old age was all he desired. Would he ever find peace in this cursed valley?

Like a derisive echo of his thoughts he heard the shots. There were three shots and they were spaced like some sort of signal. They were like a part of his half-dream – Then the voice called and he knew it was no dream. The voice called again harshly, terrible, called his name. *Brad Turner! Brad Turner!* – He rebuttoned his clothes with frantic haste and grabbed his gun from his belt. As he ran down the stairs there were more shots; then the voice called again shrilly, rising to a scream which had no words, no meaning.

The shots, the voice, they had come from behind the ranchhouse. But now there was nothing, nothing at all, and Brad slowed down as he went through the kitchen. He flattened himself against the wall as he looked out of the window. It was lighter out there but he could see nothing except the old familiar things.

He moved across to the door and stood there for a moment, listening. He lifted the latch and opened the door a little. He listened again. All he heard was the soughing of the night wind from the hills and, faint in the distance, the restless lowing of cattle. He opened the door wider and eased his body through.

Outside, he began to move along the wall, staring out into the darkness. He saw the flashes, felt a blow in his shoulder; the reports seemed to sound in his ears. He had been slammed back against the wall by the force of the slug; now he felt himself slipping. He fell forward on his belly, saw more flashes directly in front of him, heard the slugs *thunk* into the wall behind him. He tried to bring his gun forward to raise it. 'Fool,' he muttered savagely. '*Fool.*'

He thought he heard shouts and running footsteps. The gun was too heavy for him and was slipping from his hand, the night was getting darker, darker – the black night closed in around him and over him—

When he came to his senses he was lying on his back and somebody was bending over him. He struck out feebly. 'Hold it, Brad,' said a voice. 'Hold it.'

'Nevada,' he said weakly: 'That skunk – who was it?'

'It looks like he got away, old friend. But don't worry, he didn't get you. Just a punctured shoulder is all you've got. You'll be as good as new in no time.'

Another figure came down beside Brad: 'He got away all right,' said Tim Greer. 'If only I'd had my horse saddled—' He broke off as Nevada said, 'Gimme a hand to get him upstairs.'

Men were running around in the yard; there was a lot of shouting going on. As the partners laid Brad down he said, 'There was somebody else down there – didn't you hear the voice, screaming?

'I didn't hear any screaming,' said Tim, 'only the shooting.'

'Somebody shouted my name. Then they screamed—'

'To call you out, to make you run into it.'

'No! Nobody could scream like that unless something had happened to them. There's somebody else out there I tell yuh!'

'All right, Brad, don't upset yourself—'

'I'll go,' said Tim. 'And I'll send one of the boys for the doctor.'

In the yard he almost ran into Matt Jarando who said he had already sent for a medico. Tim said

Nevada could handle things till then but Jarando said he'd go up anyway and he ran into the house.

'Keep searching, boys,' said Tim as he approached a knot of men. 'Boss's orders – he thinks there's still somebody out here.'

Many of the men seemed scared to leave their fellows. They all had guns in their hands and they milled like sheep. Tim was scared one of them might start shooting at the shadows. He began to walk in a straight line from the spot where Turner had been shot. He reached the remains of a tumbledown outhouse which would not have sheltered a rabbit. Every morning the cook used parts of it for firewood; pretty soon there would be nothing left. Tim explored around there. It was too dark to look for shells though he figured this was where the bushwacker had lain. However, there was no hide nor hair of anything.

He moved over to the right, and reached a buckboard which was jacked up while undergoing repairs. He skirted this and almost fell over the bundle on the ground. He went down on one knee and rolled the thing over. It was a man all right – and he seemed to be pretty dead.

Tim was scared to show a light in case one of his own pardners started shooting at him so he shouted, 'Hey, fellers! Over here.'

They came a-running. Then he took out his lucifers and made a flame. He cupped it in his hands and held it over the face of the fallen man. The features were illuminated garishly, black and white like those of a china doll. A memory struggled in Tim's head; then the match went out.

He struck another. He saw again the round face, the eyes bulging, the lips distended in terror and pain, the black quiff of hair. Another man echoed the name which groped for utterance in Tim's brain.

'It's Gowans, that Chicago agent fellow.'

Yes, it was Gowans all right. And his back was riddled with bullets.

CHAPTER ELEVEN

The doc pronounced Brad Turner out of danger. He suggested sending to Kansas City for a trained nurse but Julia Lakeman stepped in and said she would handle everything. The doc was glad to let her do so: here was just another example of how the menfolk around here depended on this young woman.

Nolly Travers and Bill Lakeman came hotfoot and Brad held council in his bedroom. At first it had been thought that some vengeful cowhand with a bee in his bonnet had killed Gowans. But why shoot at Brad Turner too? Was it because the man had been afraid of pursuit and wanted to nip it in the bud at the outset.

It was shrewd old Bill Lakeman who suggested the more probable explanation: that Gowans had been coming to the ranch to tell Turner something and had been shot to keep his mouth shut. Then the killer, who had been a daring fellow had waited for Brad to appear.

'But what would Gowans want to tell me?' said Brad a little querulously. 'The only reason he could come here would be in order to make me another offer.'

'He made nobody else an offer,' said Nolly Travers. 'In fact I thought he had fled the country.'

'So did I,' said Lakeman.

'Maybe this ties the Ace people up with this jamboree after all.'

'Maybe.'

So, on the note of another 'maybe', the ranchers took their leave.

Pete Lagrue was the next visitor on the list. He came alone but not long afterwards Brad sent for Nevada and Tim. When they arrived Lagrue was still standing there beside the bed. Brad gave his orders succintly and without explanation. He told the two pardners to ride out with Lagrue, to go where he took them and do as he said. As they were leaving the room he made a very cryptic remark. 'I guess you're the only two boys who'll give Pete an even chance.'

As they were riding out they met Matt Jarando. When he asked gruffly what they were about, Lagrue told him they were just going to do a little chore for the boss.

Jarando said, 'If you're gonna try and track the skunk who did last night's shooting I'm afraid you're gonna have a disappointment, I found some tracks,' he pointed, 'going that way, towards the hills. But the man must have ridden right through the herd and where he went after that no one knows.'

THE BISHOP RIDERS

'Maybe we'll scout up in them hills anyway,' said Lagrue.

Jarando's face was dispassionate. 'Suit yourself,' he said and shrugged and went on his way.

The three men made a bee-line for the hills and Lagrue finally led them into the mouth of the Widow Pass. More by way of making conversation than anything else Nevada said: 'This place ain't used much.'

'We came through this way when we first entered the territory,' Tim added.

'Yeh, because it was a short cut. But the other pass is always used by the folks hereabouts. As you know the Widow is very narrow. She's also very dangerous, allus tossing rocks down on unwary wayfarers.'

Lagrue said. 'But if a man wanted to enter the valley quickly and without being seen this is the way he'd come isn't it? '

'Yeh, I guess so.'

'All right, let's not gab any more. Let's just ride and keep our eyes peeled.'

Lagrue was mighty bossy all of a sudden: an angry retort rose to Tim's lips but he choked it back as Nevada gave him a warning look.

The rock walls towered each side of them and the little used track was bumpy beneath the horses' feet. Here and there stunted vegetation sprang from cracks in the rock door or clung limpet-like to the walls. In some parts of the pass the walls bulged at the top. They were knobbly: they certainly looked loose and perilous.

'Take care here.' warned Nevada.

They went around a slight bend. The horses slipped and slithered, and snorted a little. At one point they had to go in single file to get past a fantastic-looking outcrop of rocks. The sky was a narrow strip of blue above and down here they moved in a kind of twilight. It was an eerie atmosphere and the horses did not like it at all. The men were silent, as if reluctant to join their voices to the echoes which their horses' hoofs had already awakened.

Lagrue led the way, going very slowly, looking at the ground around him all the while, leaning forward with his head bent like an Indian scout. The pass widened a little again. There was more vegetation, a tangled patch of it to the right of them. Then, with another abrupt change of terrain another tall fantastic outcrop of rock almost blocked the way up ahead.

'Is that fresh?' said Tim pointing.

'No, son,' said Nevada. 'That outcrop's been part of the scenery around here for more years than I can remember.'

'That 'ud made it pretty old!'

'Wait a minute,' said Lagrue sharply. He wheeled his horse towards the patch of vegetation. He dismounted and ploughed through the outer ring. The partners followed him. In the middle of the ring of vegetation was an oblong patch of sand and face downwards there lay the body of a man.

An involuntary cry broke from Tim. 'The sheriff!'

Yes, there was no mistaking those beautiful clothes, although they were now a rumpled and bloodstained mockery on the slack, dead figure.

Sheriff Francis Lord had been shot in the back. Gently Lagrue rolled him over. His eyes were closed, his face was as handsome as ever and almost peaceful. The buzzards had not gotten to him yet: maybe even they feared to enter this cleft in the hills.

The Sheriff's right hand had been stretched out before him and even after his position had been changed it pointed upwards like the finger of doom. 'Look,' said Tim suddenly. 'He's been scratching here.'

The three men gathered before the pointing finger and bent to discover the message the dying man, his blood already spotting the sand, had tried to write among those shifting grains.

Aloud Tim Greer spelled out: 'N – O – then there's a break. I can't make anything out of those scratches – But wait a minute – over here.' His fingers traced a pattern above the ground. 'A – C – E – Ace – Then another space and a letter all on its own: B – The poor guy got kinda desperate here. You can see where his fingers clutched and scratched. I guess he couldn't make it any more. We've got 'No Ace B – and that's all!'

'Hundred to one the Ace part refers to the Ace Development people,' said Lagrue. 'That's why the sheriff went away: to investigate those Ace people.

There's his answer, though it's a little hard to understand. Either no company actually exists, or Lord couldn't get a line on them, or discover any proof that they were mixed up with the Bishop's Riders. What the B stands for I can't think – unless it's B for Bishop. Hank was game to the last but he just couldn't finish the chore this time.'

The other two men looked at the gunman curiously. He seemed to know so much, also this was the first time they had heard the sheriff referred to as 'Hank'. Lagrue rose, ignoring their questioning gaze. He went on along the pass to the outcrop of rock which almost blocked it up ahead. When Tim and Nevada reached him he was down on his knees and holding two cartridge shells in the palm of his hand.

'Winchester repeater,' he said. 'And – look – here's the toemarks of the man's boots. He must have kneeled down here in concealment. He waited till Hank had gone by, then he shot him in the back – he didn't take any chances.'

They scouted around but found no more clues. They didn't even discover the place where the dry-gulch merchant had stashed his horse and that puzzled them a little.

'Maybe he left it hidden at the other end of the pass,' said Lagrue.

'But wouldn't that be risky? Wouldn't he be scared of the beast calling the sheriff's horse and giving itself away, a thing it probably wouldn't do if its master was near it?'

They went to the other end of the pass. Again they found no tracks or clues of any kind. They retraced their steps and Lagrue laid the body of Francis Lord across the front of his saddle. As they rode back towards *Snake W* range the lean gunman began to tell his story.

For the last couple of years his gun had been hired out to the Government: he was a State Marshal. Stranger things happened in the lawless West; many desperadoes with fast reps, sometimes through no direct fault of their own, had in their search for vindication or adventure gone over to the other side of the fence. The gun was law and they were its exponents. Sheriff Francis Lord, known to his Texas intimates as 'Dandy Hank' was in reality a Deputy Marshal and, when the Bishop's Riders began their games, he had sent to headquarters for help.

'Hank might've acted like a conceited ass,' said Lagrue. 'It was part of his pose – but he was a first-rate man who knew his own limitations. Headquarters sent me along. I rode in haphazardly, pretending to be an ordinary cowhand – which wasn't hard to do, believe me, gentlemen. I wasn't sure what I was going to do. Well you know what happened – and Brad Turner hired me. A little later I played a long shot and told him who I really was and in what capacity. Also Hank and I got together – with the result that Hank went out to do this chore.' Lagrue's voice became a little hoarse. 'I'll get the guy who did this, if it's the last thing I do.'

He seemed glad to talk, as if he could not bear to be silent, as if, now that he had once started, he wanted to get it all off his chest. They were approaching the end of the pass and could see a patch of range shimmering before them and he was still talking, when things began to happen. A rumbling noise from above, almost like thunder, gave them their first hint that things were amiss. Nevada and Tim both looked upwards but the usually so taciturn Lagrue was still gabbing.

'Look out!' yelled Tim. 'Falling rock!'

He swerved his horse and rode it against Lagrue's. The man came alive, his sudden change of demeanour was almost miraculous. 'Under the lip!' he yelled. 'Get under the lip!' – which was what old-stager Nevada was already doing. They pulled their horses sideways, hard against the rockface and gentled them with hands and soothing voices.

A huge boulder fell first, alone, bringing with it a shower of dust. Then the smaller stuff began to come, though most of it was big enough to kill a man. Then there was a regular avalanche and the rock wall tumbled. The whole pass was full of thunder and dust that was like a thick yellow fog.

The three men could only vaguely see each other. Dust made their eyes smart and their throats tingle. They coughed and sneezed. Flying chips of rock stung their faces. Tim Greer raised his fingers to his forehead and felt the blood running stickily from his scalp. Nevada cursed as something which felt like a hornet stung him in the arm. He reached up and plucked forth a sliver of rock like a tiny thin-bladed knife. One of the horses attempted to bolt and screamed with fear and pain as flying rocks buffetted its head. The three men had their work cut out to quiet the frightened beast.

The rumbling up above slowly became less. The echoes rolled away over the hills. The tiny shale fell like rain. Then the dust began to drift away and the three men found their way blocked by a huge heap of rock and rubble.

They climbed over this, pulling their horses, with much cajoling and threats, after them. Tim Greer was the last to make the laborious trip. He stood atop of the miniature mountain and looked upwards. There was very little lip left on the top there now and he knew that if the stuff had fallen much longer the overhanging piece which had been their protection would have come with it. And they wouldn't have stood a chance. The craggy walls and the jagged lip outlined against the dust-speckled sky told him nothing. But he wondered what had caused all those tons of rock to come tumbling down. Could it have been human agency? Or was he just a naturally suspicious young cuss? He left the question in the air, he did not even voice it as he joined his pards.

Not until they were safely out of the pass did they check up on the damage. 'It could have been worse,' was Nevada Jenkins' philosophic comment.

The stream of Lagrue's eloquence had been dammed. They were approaching the ranch before he spoke anything more than monosyllables. Then as the white buildings, so peaceful in the sunlight, hove in sight he said, 'Everybody knows I'm Pete Lagrue, the Texas killer—' There was a bitter quirk to his lips, 'but the only persons who know I'm a lawman are Brad Turner and you two. I want you to keep it under your hat.'

'We already intended to do that,' said Tim Greer curtly.

Lagrue smiled thinly. 'Maybe I ought not to've mentioned it,' he said. 'Sorry.' Then he went on, 'People mustn't know the full facts about Hank Lord. We were following a couple of strays when we found him lying in the pass. That's all. I guess us, being strangers, and me particularly because of my rep will be suspected—'

'We can stand it,' said Tim. Then he grinned wryly: there was still something about this phlegmatic killer which he could not help liking.

The ranch was very quiet, almost too quiet. Tim was surprised at the relief he felt when, at last, Brad Turner, his arm in a sling, came down the verandah steps. His face was bleak and looked very old; he drooped a little as he came towards them and they knew that they had no need to tell him what the result of their chore had been; in his despair he already knew.

CHAPTER TWELVE

Later he rode with the three men and they took the body into town. Their arrival caused a stir, even in the somnolent early afternoon. The sheriff's deputy, Cal Stevens, listened to their tale in silence, his bleak eyes looking from one to the other of them. He had liked Francis Lord, probably he was the only one in town who had really understood the worth of the man. They did not tell him about the scribble in the dust, which Lagrue had obliterated with one sweep of his hand, but they gave him the Winchester shells.

'A lot of use these will be,' he said, his voice unnaturally high. 'I'll take a couple of men and go and look around out there.' His eyes seemed to go darker as he watched them, waiting for one of them to speak again.

Nevada Jenkins said, 'Be careful, son. The Widow's getting mighty fractious, she had a shot at burying us under a rock-slide.'

'Pity she didn't bury the skunk who did this,'

said Stevens cryptically. He shrugged. 'I'll go get the undertaker's men.'

The news got around fast. Already a small crowd was forming outside the office and there were little knots of people in different parts of the street. Lagrue suggested a drink so they entered the *Peterborough Saloon*. It was pretty full of chattering people but the confused murmur noticeably died when the four men entered. Tim Greer and Pete Lagrue, quite an imposing pair, walked shoulder to shoulder, leading the way to the bar. This was the first time Greer had been in the *Peterborough* so he looked around him boldly. He would have been surprised had anybody told him that his demeanour was arrogant.

The looks that returned his own were not friendly. Of late Bancoville was mighty shy of strangers. Greer amused himself by staring people out until they dropped their eyes. How he hated the petty suspicious atmosphere of these little cowtowns and the kind of people who lounged around in them, not cowhands, not anything really useful as far as he could see. Still, he had to admit that the folks of Trinity Valley had plenty to be suspicious about. As he bellied up to the bar he even grinned a little. But nobody grinned back. Folks said 'Howdy' to Brad Turner, who had followed his men into the saloon without protest and in a rather bemused manner. None of the voices carried the usual gaiety of a bar-room greeting. Folks were taking their drinking seriously right now; and they had plenty of things to mull over in their heads and roll from the ends of their tongues.

The lull in the conversation did not last long. Afterwards it became louder and almost unnaturally bright, particularly from the people in the immediate vicinity of the three strangers. Lagrue ordered four ryes. Both he and Greer took theirs and turned about, leaning with their backs against the bar and surveying the room in the time-honoured way. They had the gall, the aplomb which allowed them to do so without being outfaced.

Tim spotted the rowdy knot of men in the corner. They stood out from the rest of the company: they were cowhands. One or two of them made signs of greeting to Brad Turner, but, it seemed to Tim, with rather ill-grace. Nevada and Brad, with their heads bent over the bar, were talking. Tim heard the latter say something about '*Circle U* men'. Was that what the bunch were? They looked like they had been doing quite a lot of drinking.

Another man came into the saloon and went across to the bunch. He was a big man with a cast in one eye and a thick black moustache. He began talking fast. Looks were shot at the four men against the bar. Suddenly a big redheaded fellow rose, swaying a little, and shouted:

'It suttinly is time we did somep'n.'

All eyes were turned upon him. He threw out his chest and left the table. One of his pards said,

'Wait a minute, Clem,' and plucked at his sleeve. With a snarl the big fellow shook off the detaining hand. His eyes were almost hidden under shaggy red brows as he started forward. It was plain to everybody where he was bound for: people began to move away from the bar.

A couple more men rose and followed at a discreet distance behind the redheaded Clem. The talking died; it was as if there had never been any clatter and cursing and gossip, everything was crystallized into this moment, this fragile stillness broken only by the sibilant shuffling of feet on sawdusted boards. Clem was not staggering any more. He seemed to be cold sober, his huge body swelling with some secret rage.

Men started as Clem spoke suddenly, harshly. 'We've got a killer from Texas amongst us, folks – an' the sheriff's been murdered – an' it was the killer from Texas who brought him in if you please—'

'What's eating you, Clem?' said Brad Turner mildly, but the big fellow ignored him. Somebody had been talking; pretty soon it would be all over town: already faces were pressed to the window of the saloon as people gawped at the Texas gunman and the man who confronted him.

Clem had a well-developed sense of the dramatic, in drink and rage it had mellowed and given him a righteous sense of indignation too. He flung out a hand and pointed it at the lean cold-eyed man against the bar.

'There he stands. Pete Lagrue! The great Pete Lagrue, the hired murderer who's never been beaten yet. Men like him are responsible for what is going on in this territory right now. Because of him men are scared to go out in the dark and women and kids aren't safe in their own homes—'

A voice behind him said softly, 'Come away, Clem.'

He did not heed it. Brad Turner said: 'You're crazy, Clem. What do you—'

The big man's harsh voice cut him short. 'You keep out o' this. All of you, keep out of it. Move aside and let this buzzard speak for himself.'

'Better do as he says,' said Pete Lagrue softly.

The three men moved away each side of him, watching the *Circle U* boys behind Clem. The stretch of bar was empty except for the lean figure against it. There was a clear space before him and in the centre of that stood Clem. The silence seemed to stretch, until men felt like screaming, then Lagrue said, 'Get on with your spiel, friend.'

The voice came silkily from the motionless form, a soft Texas drawl which matched the half-closed languid eyes. Only Clem who was alone and nearest, could see the menace which shone in those dark slits. But Clem was one of the fastest gunnies hereabouts. Also he did not lack courage, so he did not hesitate over his reply.

'I'm all through talking, Mr Lagrue. I'm calling your hand. We don't want people like you in

Trinity Valley. I'm giving you a chance to go before I send you!'

'I was just having a quiet drink,' said the soft voice.

'Move, or draw! Draw!' Clem's voice rose to a shout. He crouched a little.

Lagrue did not even move away from the bar. He smiled a little, a mocking smile calculated to drive an angry man to the point of madness. 'Go away, big-mouth,' he drawled.

'Talk!' screamed Clem. 'Can't you do anything but talk? You call yourself the fastest gun in the West. Let's see your smoke. Draw, you son-of-a-bitch—' He stopped talking abruptly. He adopted a pose almost as nonchalant as Lagrue's. He said coolly, sneeringly, 'The fastest gun in the West. Pah!' He spat into the sawdust.

'Can I help it if men give me names?' said Lagrue, gently. 'And if other foolish men try to take those names away from me and adopt them themselves! Go away, you bigheaded fool.'

Clem did not say anything more, he moved. The action was not violent, it was just smooth and incredibly swift. Clem's gun was out of its holster when a puff of smoke blossomed from Lagrue's hip, drifting upwards like the echo of the gunshot and the reflection of the spitting flame. The force of the heavy slug spun Clem around like a top. Then he began to sink to the floor saying, 'Oh, Oh, Oh,' over and over in a treble moan.

Lagrue had not moved his position but his gun

menaced Clem's two pards. 'Get away from him,' he said. 'He ain't hurt none. He'll live. But I'll kill the next man who makes a nasty move – Back, I said, *back*!' His voice did not rise but now it was metallic.

'I'm coming through,' he said and he began to move.

'That goes for all of us,' said Tim Greer and he had his gun in his hand too.

He motioned Nevada and Brad to precede him and follow Lagrue and they did so. Brad said loudly, 'It was self defence.' Lagrue said, 'I don't need any justification.' As they reached the doors Nevada and Brad had their guns out too, menacing the still and pop-eyed crowd. 'Rush 'em!' said somebody at the back but nobdy moved.

'We'll be leaving you now,' Tim Greer shouted. 'The first man who shows his head above these batwings gets it blown off.' The batwings flapped slowly to; the men were making for their horses when Deputy Stevens came in sight. 'Hey, what's going on! Hey, wait a minute!'

'Sorry we can't stop now, Cal,' said Brad Turner and as they rode down the street Tim looked at his boss and knew that whatever had been eating the old man he had gotten over it now. There was an almost devilish twinkle in his eyes and he held his gun balanced loosely in the palm of his hand. His finger closed around the butt, his thumb tightened on the hammer. He raised the gun and fired three rapid shots into the air.

'I've always wanted to shoot up this damned burg,' he said.

Nobody tried to stop them as they thundered out onto the trail.

The range was peaceful, washed by moonlight. The ranch buildings of the *Snake W* were dazzling white, barred and patterned by shadows. There was a little breeze, and the lowing of the distant cattle was restful.

The sound of the horses' hoofs was only a faint rhythm at first but it pretty soon rose to a drumming crescendo and men began to grab their guns and come out from the bunk house. The riders swept into the yard and drew up in front of the ranchhouse. Brad Turner came out onto the verandah with a shotgun in the crook of his arm. He let the gun fall, let it dangle at the end of his arm.

'Gosh, you had me worried,' he said. 'You came kinda fast didn't you, Bill?'

The big hunch-shouldered man on the foremost horse said, 'This isn't exactly a social call, Brad.'

Turner's shot gun jerked a little in his hand. 'Oh – huh – how come!'

'A dirty gunman you're harbouring here plugged one o' my men – we aim to run him plumb out o' the territory. An' that's too good for him by rights.'

'What if I say you can't have my man – an' that mob o' yourn is trespassing on my property?'

'I was hoping you wouldn't act awkward, Brad. We sure aim to get that man.'

The two oldtimers eyed each other. Bill Lakeman was the first to move. With slow laborious movements he dismounted from his horse. Then with his eyes still on Brad he began to walk towards the verandah steps. The faces of the two elderly men were etched and pitted by the moonlight. They both looked grim but a little absent as if this was not happening to them at all but to two other fellows. Two other old jackasses who had been friends for years but who acted now like two contestants meeting for the first time. The strain had wrought a change in them, the evil had reached out and touched them.

Bill Lakeman walked slowly, with wider strides than was his wont, his old back bent but his head up, his eyes looking at Brad as if they had never seen him before. His hands hung loosely, almost ape-like at his sides and his measured tread had acquired a springiness. In his younger days Bill had had quite a fast rep as a gun-fighter. His grotesque shadow was thrown in front of him. It moved nearer to the motionless figure on the verandah until pretty soon the grotesque head was touching the other man's feet.

Then the man spoke softly. 'I shouldn't come any nearer if I were you, Bill,' and the muzzle of the shotgun was now pointing steadily at Lakeman's chest.

Lakeman stopped. 'You damn' fool,' he said,

THE BISHOP RIDERS

'My men are right behind me an' every one of 'em is armed.'

'I've got men too,' was the gentle reply. 'If anything happens to me you know that not one of you would get out of here alive, don't you!'

The *Snake W* people moved forward a little, and a man detached himself from their ranks. 'Do you want me, gentlemen?' he asked.

A voice said: 'That's him, boss. We ought to lynch the skunk. Let's take him and get out of here.'

A ripple of movement went through the ranks of both factions. They were like dogs straining at the leash; then Brad Turner's quiet voice spoke up again.

'Let you and me go inside and talk, Bill.'

Lakeman looked a little taken aback by this proposal. He was in a quandary. He didn't want to appear to backdown, but he realized, now his crusading fervour had died, that there was little else he could do except as Brad wished. Anyway, having a pow-wow was not tantamount to backing down, was it?

'All right,' he said. And as Brad lowered the shotgun his old friend mounted the steps.

The *Snake W* boss said, 'You'd better come up Pete; and Nevada, Tim and Matt—'

Bill said, 'Wait a minute. If that's the way the cards are stacked I aim to bring four of my boys in there too.'

Brad shrugged and said softly: 'All right, but

pick four you can trust – what goes on in here has to be strictly confidential.'

'Kinda mysterious aren't you?' jeered Bill. He called out four names. As his voice died away hoofs clattered in the yard. The rider made a half-circle around the mounted men and came to a halt before the house. It was Julia.

'What fool's business is this?' she cried.

Bill Lakeman stiffened. Then he whirled on his daughter. 'Don't say that! What brings you here—?'

Brad Turner broke in on his tirade. 'Light down, Julia. Come on in.'

The girl dismounted and followed the men into the house. Bill and Brad brought up the rear. They both turned before passing through the door.

Bill shouted : 'Stay put, all of yuh. Don't move until I come out an' tell you to. An' no funny business.'

'That goes for my men, too,' yelled Brad. 'Go back to the bunkhouse or your chores, all of youl'

Muttering among themselves and casting nasty glances at the visitors, the *Snake W* men drifted away. The *Circle U* boys sat their horses, outwardly stolid – but once the door had closed behind the two boss-men they began to chatter.

'We ought to've taken that skunk pronto' – 'We never ought to've come here in the first place – them two old goats are like a pair o' lovebirds.' – 'Gee, I suttinly thought there was gonna be fireworks.' – 'Clem was drunk I tell yuh – an' all he's got is a punctured shoulder.' – 'Turner never ought to've set that skunk on atall. We don't want his kind in Trinity Valley' – 'We've got enough trouble.' – 'It's my opinion he's mixed up with the Bishop's Riders.'

From the direction of the bunkhouse a jeering voice shouted, 'Ooh, look at the stuffed dummies!'

'Go boil your head,' retorted one of the better-natured *Circle U* boys. There was a little laughter on both sides. The tension was broken.

The house was blank and silent in the moonlight. Sitting his horse and looking at the closed door, the sightless windows, a man said glumly: 'What happens next?'

It was a trite remark and yet a poignant one. It was the ghost-cry, the plaint in the night, the verse and the chorus of the theme-song of Trinity Valley.

CHAPTER THIRTEEN

The *Circle U*'s raid on the *Snake W* turned out to be a complete flop – which, strangely enough, as ultimately almost everybody had to admit, was the best thing for all concerned. Bill Lakeman made no comment as to the possible fate of Pete Lagrue and, in view of Bill's moody and explosive nature nobody broached the subject though the general opinion was that Miss Julia, who rode so straight and still beside her father had in some way 'swung it'. She was a dandy little fixer that gal, even if a man did not always see eye to eye with her.

So another night passed and the morning came again and the range smiled in the sunshine. The evil pall seemed to have been lifted and the cowhands joshed each other and hoped that the Bishop had gone back to hell. But the range ceased to smile as twilight fell and a drizzle of rain came with it. Then a black night followed and the rain was lashed to fury by a driving, moaning wind.

Pete Lagrue was returning from a visit to deputy Cal Stevens in town when he was bushwacked from behind a rocky outcrop along the trail. His horse was shot from under him and, as he rolled, bullets spat viciously all around, but he snaked into a patch of scrub and lay still. He saw the silhouette of a wide-brimmed sombrero, and he shot at it. The sombrero disappeared. A few seconds later hoofs clattered, fading away in the distance as a cursing Lagrue staggered to his feet. He took the saddle from the dead beast and began the long walk home. He had a horror of walking; of being caught in the darkness without his horse, of being ridden down. He looked warily around him as the miles went by wearily beneath his scuffed high-heeled riding boots.

Nevada Jenkins and Tim Greer were members of a strong guard which circled the herd that night. It was they, fortunately, who spotted the teetering figure and recognised it. Pete Lagrue sat down on the grass, threw down his saddle, groaned as he took off his boots. Then massaging his feet tenderly and punctuating his talk with blistering curses, he told his tale.

'There's a couple of spare horses round at the tent,' said Nevada.

'Don't bother to put your boots on yet, Pete,' said Tim. 'Have my horse to ride to the tent. I'll stretch my legs.' Lagrue tucked his boots under his arm and with protestations of heartfelt gratitude mounted up. They slowly skirted the herd, greeting curious night-riders as they went along. They were dismounting at the tent when all hell broke loose.

The raiders had followed the direction of the wet blustering wind and it deadened the sound of their approach until they were almost upon the herd. The three men at the tent screamed a warning and remounted swiftly. Lagrue had never put his boots on so fast in his life. He grabbed one of the spare horses and slung his saddle on it.

The three men were partially obscured by the tent. Maybe the Riders did not see them as they veered to circle the herd. The partners opened up. Lagrue gave a blood-curdling rebel yell and charged. Two of the masked riders pitched from their horses. The hooded leader was turning his horse and shouting orders in a strangely muffled voice.

Lagrue wheeled his horse. 'Around the other way,' he yelled.

'Warn the boys,' shouted Tim Greer. The three men raced neck-and-neck.

They skirted the back of the herd and ran into the nucleus of the *Snake W* force. The bunch of Riders, racing to do their little chore of murder, suddenly found themselves outnumbered. Six of them bit the dust in the space of the same number of minutes. The rest turned and fled.

'Let 'em go,' bawled Lagrue. 'We've got to help the boys round the other end. The Bishop's there – with a bigger force.'

The cowhands turned about. They went around the head of the herd. They could hear the firing now, fast and furious. A man cried out hoarsely. The sound rose to a scream then died. The newcomers broke upon a scene of milling horses. The only way they could tell friend from foe was by the masks the latter wore.

It seemed the Riders had not bargained for this sudden attack from reinforcements. Many of them broke away, began to run. The leader could be heard bawling frenziedly, though his words were uncertain, muffled by the hood. Tim Greer took a snapshot at him and saw his hat spin from his head. Then the Bishop was lying flat over his horse's neck. The beast streaked away from the scene of battle. Tim set his horse at a gallop. A masked figure loomed up in front of him. Their horses met with a terrific impact and Tim felt himself falling. Then he was rolling amid flying hoofs. One caught him a glancing blow on the temple and, for a moment everything was hazy.

The leaders of the herd, scared by the shooting were beginning to move. The sluggish mass of steers gathered speed. Cowhands galloped up front, shooting right and left. They nipped the stampede in the bud but, in the interim the Bishop and his men had gotten a good start.

Riding furiously, following the sound of distant hoofbeats with which the wind played tricks the *Snake W* men found themselves near the mouth of the Widow Pass.

'Looks like they've gone through there,' said one man.

'Naw. I don't think they'd risk it,' said another.

It was Pete Lagrue and his two partners who led the bunch forward into the pass. It was pitch-black here: the ideal place for an ambush. 'Dismount,' hissed Lagrue. 'Hug the walls.'

The men obeyed his orders mechanically, without question. They moved in Indian file along one side of the pass. Every man's nerves were stretched like fiddle-strings. Their eyes ached as they stared into the darkness. But the attack, when it came, and if it could be called an attack, did not come from out there. There was a rumbling up above which Tim Greer understood only too well. It was he who yelled. 'Make a bolt for it, there's a fall starting!'

Men mounted frenziedly, turning their mounts about. The horses did not need any urging, scared by the rapidly-growing volume of sound they galloped madly. The rocks began to fall around the fleeing men and beasts. The dust almost blinded them but the deafening roar behind told them that they had escaped the main fall.

They gathered in a knot at the mouth of the pass. Except for cuts and bruises there was not much damage done.

'I wouldn't go back in there for a king's ransom,' said one man feelingly.

'I guess it wouldn't be much use anyway,' said Pete Lagrue.

THE BISHOP RIDERS

They went back to the herd which, although milling restlessly, now showed no inclination to bolt. The wind had dropped a little; the air was full of damp and the moon was struggling to dodge past scudding clouds.

'They didn't have time to take their dead and wounded with them this time,' said Lagrue.

Already men had dismounted and were searching for friend as well as foe. Luckily, the only bullet-casualty in the *Snake W* ranks was a man who had crawled to the shelter of the tent. He had a bullet in his thigh but had managed to staunch the blood with his neckerchief. A couple of men took him back to the ranch, while the rest carried on with their search. Nevada Jenkins heard the death-rattle in a man's throat as he bent over him.

More of the boys clustered near. A match was struck. Nobody knew the dead man. 'Too bad,' said Nevada. 'He might have talked.'

They found two more dead strangers. They stood a little longer around a third body. In the flickering light Tim Greer said 'I'm sure I've seen that gink before.' 'Me too,' said another man. Tim's brain knocked like it was missing a cog: there was a memory he could not quite grasp. The match went out and another one was struck, the sickly yellow light illuminating the big face with the black bar of moustache. The man's eyes were open, turned upwards horribly, but it was plain to see he had a cast in one of them.

Suddenly Tim remembered; he wondered if

anybody else had remembered – but if they had, like him, they did not speak. He remembered the saloon, the knot of truculent *Circle U* boys, the big man who came in and spoke to them and, it seemed, precipitated the attack on Pete Lagrue. That big man now lay dead here: why had he, an employee of Bill Lakeman, ridden with the Bishop?

The next morning a party of men explored the Widow Pass, only to find that it had been blocked by the latest landslide. They found nothing of interest; they returned to the ranch.

They reported that a lot of the nesters seemed to be leaving the valley. There was a spirit of brooding over the range; men, instead of being overjoyed because a victory had been scored over the Bishop, seemed to move in a fatalistic half-daze.

Halfway through the morning Pete Lagrue rode away from the ranchhouse on some secret chore. Matt Jarando also rode out alone to see how his riders were getting on. Just after he had gone Nevada and Tim presented themselves at the ranchhouse. They told Brad, who had great faith in his old friend, and the hard-faced young man who was his side-kick, that they were going into the hills.

The partners set out. They did not seem to be in any hurry. They meandered around the herd and spoke to a couple of hands. Then they kind of sidled away. Only when they were out of sight of the herd did they set their horses at a gallop. They approached the Widow Pass from the side, skirting the ashes of the Gaynor homestead where young Tony, who now had a wooden memorial erected to him in Bancoville's Boot Hill, had made his last glorious stand.

'This reign of terror,' said Nevada. 'There's a kind of reason behind it – but the reason, I should say of a man whose brain is slightly unhinged.'

The old man was in one of his rare talkative moods. Which meant that he had something buzzing around in his noddle and, maybe, when it had crystalized properly he would give it tongue. So Tim kept silent and listened to the pearls of wisdom which trickled from time to time from his partner's lips.

They moved into the Widow Pass. They halted at the sloping wall of rock and rubble which blocked their way. Nevada said, 'The boys didn't think it would be worth while to try and get through that – D'yuh think we could get past it, Tim?'

'I think we could get over it.' They dismounted. The young man paced along the base of the rock-pile and looked upwards until he had to squint his eyes against the watery sun. It seemed to him that the fall had widened the pass considerably at this point, there was almost a gap up there, there was quite a decent light to work by. He climbed a little, testing the rock for firmness and footholds. Finally he called Nevada.

They climbed silently. Nevada's chatter had left

him for a while. He climbed like a mountain-goat. Not until they halted on the top did he speak and then it was only as if he was thinking aloud. 'I useter know this territory pretty well. Probably better than Brad Turner and Bill Lakeman. I useter explore these hills with a friendly old Injun called Leaping Cloud. He knew all the secret trails. I was only a little shaver but I remember now as if it was only yesterday.' He sighed and there were a whole heap of 'yesterdays' in that sigh. 'Well, come on,' he went on. 'I ain't gettin' any younger standing here.'

As they began to descend on the other side of the pile they realized that the slide had fetched great chunks out of the rock walls so that the pass seemed to be pitted with small caves and fissures.

'I had a hunch—'

'Come again, oldtimer,' said Tim but Nevada did not seem to hear him, his keen eyes were raking the rock walls. They reached the uneven floor and Nevada was still acting like an old hound-dog on the scent.

Tim stumbled along, bringing up the rear now. With his eyes he traced the rock walls upwards, they were pockmarked and tortured, they looked evil and unsafe. The Widow had a very malicious nature – it was written all over her face. Consequently, when Tim got his eyes back on the level he was not too surprised to find that his pardner had vanished; he had a fleeting thought, of a kind unusual to him, that the spirits had finally gotten hold of Nevada and taken him from human ken.

He looked towards a clump of battered and dusty vegetation and called softly 'Nevada!' and the rock walls echoed his voice derisively; they played with the sound until it was a tortured moan fading into the narrow sky above.

A spectral voice said, 'I had an idea them falls would uncover some of the old passages.'

Tim charged forward and broke through the tangle of scrub. Darkness enveloped him. He recoiled involuntarily as a hand clutched his arm. 'Careful,' said Nevada. 'Follow me.'

Light filtered in around them; Tim followed his partner's stooping back. The passage began to widen and he had a glimpse of the sky again. He was unaccountably relieved; he had been ashamed of the panic which had swelled up in his breast as he traversed that coffin-like passage in the rock. He pushed forward almost eagerly as they turned a slight bend, their scrabbling footsteps awakening the echoes. The fact that he blundered into the old man and almost sent him on his knees, probably saved Nevada's life for, as they turned the bend, the report of a gun rattled among the rock walls. The slug whined and ricochetted; the echoes shattered. The two men took cover.

CHAPTER FIFTEEN

Up on the sloping walls a man seemed to be climbing like a fly. Tim took a snapshot at him and missed.

'If he gets up top there he'll be able to keep us at bay forever,' said Tim. 'Cover me, oldtimer.' He ran forward and began to climb.

The man above, who wore a hat which looked much too big for his head, turned and saw his danger and began shooting. From down below Nevada retaliated. The hat spun from the man's head and floated past Tim like some grotesque bat. The man made a desperate spurt and slipped. He slid, his arms waving frenziedly. Tim flattened himself against the rock: he did not want to be bowled over by a hurtling body. The man grabbed on again but, after his narrow escape, he had lost a margin of his lead. Tim climbed fast: Nevada didn't do any more shooting for fear of hitting his pard.

The quarry reached the end of his climb and suddenly disappeared. Tim put on a spurt and reached the crest. Slowly he raised his head. He gaped into space. He looked down at a narrow strip of grassland and saw a few steers. There was no sign of his quarry but looking to the right he saw that a ledge overlooked this tiny coffin-like valley and, perched on a wider part of it up ahead, stood a large log cabin.

Tim climbed over knobbly rocks and let himself dangle. He hung for a breathless second then let himself drop. He landed on all fours, thinking that this was a hell of a front door to use. Nevada had certainly stumbled onto something through following his hunch.

Tim knew his rear was covered by the sharp-shooting old cuss, so, without hesitation, he went on along the ledge. It widened suddenly and he saw the man. The fellow was almost as surprised, his hand flew to his hip. Tim leapt. The man, a Mexican, went down before him, spitting and clawing like a cat. They rolled and grappled for the gun. They were very near the edge of the ledge. Tim saw the world spinning crazily around him and struck out savagely. His opponent suddenly went limp. Tim looked over the edge to the grass below then slowly eased the other's unconscious body away from him. He got the man under the armpits and dragged him into a rock fissure out of sight of the silent cabin. Surely if anybody was there the ruckus would have warned them – but, anyway, he was taking no chances.

He heard a sound from the other direction and whirled, his gun leaping to his hand. He peered around the corner and saw Nevada approaching warily. He hissed a warning to him and motioned him into cover.

The Mexican was coming round as they looked down at him. Pesoes and golden dollars were sewn down the seams of his trousers and on his embroidered vest. His eyes opened and rolled; they darkened with fear as they gazed upwards at the two men with their levelled guns.

'Don't kill me, *señores*,' he said huskily.

Nevada smiled grimly, leaned forward and pointed the gun directly at the man's face. He said, 'What's in the cabin?'

'Nothing. Eet is empty now.' The man's hands fluttered. 'Don't kill me,' he parroted. He sat up.

Nevada jerked the gun. 'We'll make a deal with you. We'll let you go if you'll tell us who the Bishop is.'

The man's eyes became more fearful still, became almost round with superstitious awe. He shook his head mutely.

Nevada shrugged, smiled and lifted the gun. Sweat was beaded like tiny silver coins on the Mexican's forehead. He broke – with a hoarse scream. 'I'll tell! I'll tell!'

There was the boom of a gun at close quarters and a gasping cry came from his lips. He clutched at his chest and fell back.

'Drop the guns,' said a bass voice.

The partners were not suicidal fools: with alacrity they let the guns fall, then turned to face the man in the long black hood who came slowly forward, the Colt in his hand still smoking. Behind him was another man, his face masked, his tall body draped in a long white slicker. The leader said, 'It's a great pity, isn't it? But maybe I'll tell you who the Bishop is before you die.'

'I've got a purty good idea right now,' said Nevada.

A muffled chuckle came from the incongruous black sack headpiece. The eyes glowed strangely through the slits. The boxed-in voice said, 'If you know any prayers you'd better—' He broke off with a hoarse cry as the figure at his feet moved and two clawlike hands grabbed his legs and pulled. He was already staggering as his thumb came down on the hammer. The shot echoed and the slug whined away into nothingness. Nevada sprang forward; they wrestled for the gun as the man on the ground expired with a great rattling sigh.

The masked man in the slicker, fearful of hitting his partner, began to dance around. Tim Greer dived for the gun on the ground and even as his fingers closed on the butt a slug almost took his ear off. He was firing almost blindly as he straightened up. The man squealed as his gun looped from his hand. He clutched his arm and then, as Tim dived forward, turned and ran. The two struggling men swayed in the young man's path; Nevada went sprawling before a haymaker from the hooded man. Tim whirled and levelled his gun. There was murder in his eyes as he snarled, 'All right – back up!'

The hooded man raised his hands. Nevada rose, retrieving his gun. 'Thanks, pard,' he said. 'Now tear that fancy dress off'n him. I'll keep him covered.'

Tim ripped the black clothing savagely away and stared into the livid face of blond-haired Nolly Travers, boss of the *Big Bend* Ranch.

'A – ah,' said Nevada. 'An' I suppose this poor greaser at our feet is 'Peso' Maroni who was supposed to've been killed when the Riders 'raided' your place the night before my pard an' me turned up. Peso, who was supposed to've been buried. I thought it was kinda strange you puttin' him under the ground so quickly.'

'You're mighty clever, oldtimer.'

'I ain't been clever enough. If I had I might've stopped a lot of grief. If my memory 'ud been better I might have remembered the location of a lot of the old Indian passages. So this is the hide-out. You could do a bit of brand-blotting here I guess. But what did you do with the rest of the cattle?'

Nolly shrugged. He might have been conducting a leisurely conversation with a friend. 'We took a risk an' drove 'em right through the Widow – I've got a buyer in the next State. The young unmarked stuff I gave my own brand and let run with my own stock.'

He chuckled. 'Right under your very noses. An' I even hired a few of my neighbours' men. Most of my Riders, however, except for a batch of my own men, were strange gunnies, they camped right here. I sent 'em packing last night – you'll have a job to catch up with them now.' He chuckled again. 'I muffed my last hand—'

'You certainly did, Nolly. But go on, feller, an' you can walk as you tell us some more. Take us through the other entrance – I know there's bound to be one – an' you can walk in front, just in case.' Nevada spoke gently as if he was talking to a fractious child and, almost mechanically, Nolly began to walk.

The Ace Development Company had been his idea. His desire had been to turn the whole of Trinity Valley into one big cattle spread with huge luxurious main buildings and himself as the dictator of it all. But when his secret agent, Gowans, met with opposition he had to think up another scheme.

It was then that the teaching of his foster father, Nevada's old friend, 'Gimpy', came in handy, in a way that would have made the staunch old pioneer turn in his grave. Many a time 'Gimpy' had recounted the legend of the Bishop's Riders to the boy Nolly. He had also shown the boy secret passages and hideouts it was thought that the Riders had used. Here was a beautiful set-up, ready made for the scheming young rancher. He did not bargain for the return of Nevada Jenkins, probably the only other man who knew anything of the secret trails.

Recounted by the handsome blond-haired man it was the scheme of a megalomaniac, and as he told it now, he became lost in his grandiose dreams and his voice died to a mumble. He recounted the tale over and over to himself and nobody else could hear it any more. Questions as to the identity of his accomplices in Trinity Valley received no answer; even threats were of no avail. He led the two men to where his horse was tethered at the end of a passage. At the other end they broke through a cunning screen of creepers and found themselves in the pass again close by the place where the partners had stashed their own horses. They got them, and mounted. It was then that Nolly played his last card: the Joker which in his madness he had had up his sleeve all the time. He petrified his captors with a scream the like of which they had never heard before from beast or man, then he bolted.

Yes, he just dropped spurs to his horse and galloped away.

They told him to stop and he paid no heed. They screamed at him but he galloped on, they raised their guns together and grimly thumbed the hammers.

The Bishop pitched from his horse, which went careering onwards. The echoes of the shots died to a derisive murmur. Tim put the body across the front of his own horse and they went on.

THE BISHOP RIDERS

*

When a big force of riders surrounded the *Big Bend* Ranch later that day they met with a little resistance from a bunch of the bad boys who hadn't been able to get away in time and had entrenched themselves in a barn. The barn was set on fire and they came out with their hands up.

So far so good, but the *Snake W* people still had something over which to speculate: and this was the continued absence of Pete Lagrue. 'I said he was mixed up with that mob all along,' said one man and it took four men to prevent Tim Greer from throttling him. Tim was peeved: maybe he was peeved over his own doubts.

The next stage of the drama took place in the quiet lamplit setting of the bunkhouse. There was a poker-school under way. It was a nice night. Men, smoking and yarning passed in and out. There was still no sign of Lagrue. Matt Jarando came in and crossed the room. Tim Greer, unconsciously it seemed, thrust his feet in the foreman's path. Jarando got tangled up in them and came down heavily.

'Gosh, Matt, I'm sorry.' Tim sprang forward and helped the man to his feet. In his confused haste he was rather rough. He tore Jarando's shirt-sleeve open from shoulder to elbow, revealing the fresh white bandage on the arm beneath.

Jarando backed away, his eyes blazing. Greer

smiled gently and said, 'Had a little accident haven't you, Matt?'

Jarando's draw was a thing of wonder. His feet went slap-slap; then he had his back to the open door and was menacing everybody with the Colt. He backed through, slamming the door behind him. They heard a man cry out in pain, then Jarando's running footsteps.

Tim Greer was first at the door. He flung it open.

'Get back, you fool!' a familiar voice yelled harshly from the darkness. Then the night was hideous with gunfire; a mighty fist caught Tim in the shoulder and bowled him over; there were flashes of light, all the colours of the rainbow, then there was nothing but blackness.

He awoke to softness and coolness which was only marred a little by the throbbing ache in his shoulder. He lay in bed in the ranchhouse and Nevada Jenkins, Brad Turner, Pete Lagrue and Bill Lakeman were grinning down at him.

Nevada said: 'We plugged the hole up so's the draught won't get in. You'll be all right in a few days.'

Tim grinned. His gaze passed on to the lean gunman and he said: 'Nice to see you again, sport.'

'I'd got you guessing, huh?' retorted Lagrue. 'I went out investigating all on my lonesome. I found hoofmarks at the place where I was bushwacked last night. I suspected Jarando you see – it was just a hunch I had about the man I guess – but them hoofmarks were made by his horse all right. I checked them, then I went to take him in his cabin – a good idea that cabin, incidentally, nobody knew when he went and when he came – but he wasn't there. I was just in time to spot him going into the bunkhouse. He thought he was safe I guess.' Lagrue shrugged. 'We'ell – you know the rest.

'Jarando?' queried Tim.

'We shot things out by the barn. I guess I was a mite too good for him.' Lagrue's voice became soft and faraway. 'They always get panicky in the end an' that's what beats them.'

His voice died away and there was silence. It was broken by the sound of the opening door. Julia Lakeman came in.

'Don't overtire the patient!' she said sharply and with sly looks at the man in the bed the four visitors filed out.

Tim grinned cheekily up at his nurse. 'You just wanted to be alone with me didn't you?' he said.

Her cheeks dimpled. 'However did you guess?' Her dark eyes widened as she bent over him. Then they were closed away from his vision altogether and there was only her warm lips and the feel of her, soft yet strong, tight against him and enfolded in his arms.